APOCALYPTIC MONTESSA AND NUCLEAR LULU

A TALE OF ATOMIC LOVE

MERCEDES M. YARDLEY

Crystal Lake Publishing
www.CrystalLakePub.com

CHAPTER ONE

SHE WAS BEAUTIFUL, this woman who wandered the graveyard. All hair and eyes. In a light cotton dress covering her rounded belly, she walked barefoot across the overgrown lawns. She smiled and laughed as she touched the flowers garnishing the dead.

She saw a particularly beautiful headstone, a grave marker.

"Montessa," she read, and something about it, the strength of it, the delicacy, stopped her in her tracks. She stood and waited. Moreover, she *felt*.

"That will be your name, darling," she told the child in her womb. The newly named Montessa skipped and spun and twirled. Or perhaps she sucked her thumb in silence. Her mama couldn't really tell these days now that she was so ill. But she carried a little girl, she was sure of it, and she loved this child fiercely.

"Your life will be charmed," she said, navigating through the headstones and weeping angels as well as she could. "I believe wonderful things happen to little girls named Montessa. You're special."

Sweet thoughts. Sweet desires. But horribly, horribly unfounded. Misery and despair follows little girls named Montessa, especially little girls who are forced to go through their lives with dead mommies. Even more so when that mommy was the only one who loved them.

But she was right about one thing; Montessa was indeed special.

Montessa's shift ended at 3:00 am.

She took a shower, soaping the oils and glitter and makeup off her body. Then, she wrapped herself in a towel and used another to dry her hair. Dry enough, she pulled out her phone.

"Renan?"

"What?"

He sounded dangerous tonight. Forcibly light-hearted, so he was out with the boys, but drunk enough that he'd be mean when he came home.

"I'm off."

"What's that gotta do with me?"

"Just wondered if you were gonna pick me up, that's all."

"Not tonight. I'm doing something."

Montessa heard giggling in the background, and waited for her heart to sink and break, but nothing happened. Perhaps it had been ground to dust long ago. This was a relief.

"All right. I'll see you at home."

"Don't wait up."

"Do I ever? Goodnight."

"Hey, baby," he said. He was smiling into the phone, and she could visualize the beauty of it. Now her heart sank. Now it broke. "Who loves you?"

"You do."

"That's my girl. Be careful looks like there's a storm coming in."

"I'm always careful. Have fun, Renan."

Without the makeup, she wasn't Ruby anymore. She was just plain ole Montessa Travor. She seemed years younger when she washed away the faux confidence and sensuality, unlike some of the other girls.

Montessa put her six-inch stilettos in her purse along with her dancing costume. It didn't take much room.

Jeans and a T-shirt. Sneakers. She left out the back door, the doorman giving her a brotherly grin and a pat on the shoulder. She smiled back, her first genuine one of the day, and stepped onto the shoulder of the highway. It was four miles home, fairly straight through the Northern Nevada desert.

Montessa put her earbuds into her ears and turned on her music. Not because she particularly wanted to listen to anything, but because she didn't want to hear Renan's voice assuring her this is what it feels like to be loved.

It always hurt.

Lu watched her go.

He always watched her go.

Sitting in the trees, his back pressed against a trunk, he watched her walk home on sore feet from hours of dancing.

The boyfriend seldom came anymore. Lu didn't

mind. The guy seemed mean, hulking, treating the brunette like property, like meat, while his own eyes roved over the hips and breasts of the other dancers.

And he let the girl walk home alone for the last three nights. Stupid. You never knew what could happen to a pretty little girl.

Lu knew. It had happened several times. Several times several.

He settled back against the trees, took a cigarette, and slipped it into his mouth. He then slid his hands back into his pockets. The unlit cigarette started glowing, burning. Lu's eyes did the same as he watched the woman round the corner, disappearing from sight. He waited for a few more minutes and then walked over to his semi, parked behind the strip club. He climbed inside, laid his head back against the seat and made a decision.

He pulled out, turning onto the road. It only took a few minutes to pass the frail girl with the dancer's body. A few minutes more and he parked his semi on the soft shoulder of a curve, waiting.

Montessa tended to think too much.

At home, she constantly thought about Renan's moods, where his blows would strike if he landed them. She always wondered if he was in the mood to joke, or to ask for money, or if he would go and get high in the back room. At work, she thought about escape, about leaping off the platform and running for the door. She'd go out the back way before the bouncer could catch her, kicking off her stilettos and pelting barefoot down the street. Into the trees somewhere, living like a beast. A wild animal of wonder. She'd walk through the forest until she came out the other side, into a land of marvels.

When she walked home at night, she purposely tried not to think. She listened to her breathing, to her heartbeat, to her tender feet hitting the pavement. She felt her arms swing, her ribs move as she breathed in and out. Her body, her muscles. That was it. That was all. It was the only escape she had.

She saw a semi up ahead, gray and sleek. Normally she would have briefly wondered where it was headed, who was inside, how it would feel to walk up and ask for a ride. It didn't matter where the driver was going. In fact, she'd rather not know until it was time to wake up and stretch at her final destination. Wouldn't that be lovely? Wouldn't that be grand?

But tonight wasn't that night.

Something was . . . off.

With her eyes pinned forward, Montessa pushed her wild hair out of her face, and tried to pay attention to the music—a new playlist one of the girls at work burned for her. It was too poppy, too light, and Montessa hated it more than she thought she could ever hate anything, but it acted as a distraction.

Only three and a half more miles to go.

She blinked the burn from her eyes, dashing at them with her wrist, and then reminded herself that she never cried.

She passed the semi, her steps faltering a little before she righted herself. A little too tired, but she could push through. After all, she was her mama's daughter, and there was something special about her.

A girl like her could never give up, but just needed to keep going.

If Montessa had been paying attention, she would have noticed a shadow sliding behind her. If she had taken her earbuds out, she would have heard the surreptitious sound of sneakers on pavement, heard the sound of shallow breaths. She might have caught sight of the glint of something sinisterly sharp in the moonlight, the smell of evil deeds being considered.

None of this. None.

Montessa focused on putting one bruised foot in front of the other, on getting home so she could collapse into her bed smelling of Renan's sweat. She thought of getting something to eat, if there was anything in the house. On drinking two big glasses of cold water if there wasn't.

She focused on getting home . . . No, to the place she *lived* because it wasn't a home. It wasn't a nest. It was somewhere she paid rent and left her clothes and closed her eyes and slid under the water in the bathtub. There was no such thing as home.

She thought too much, and cursed herself mentally. Montessa bit her tongue, focusing on the steady *bop, bop, bop* of the music she endured.

A hood slid over her head. A hand clamped over her mouth. She felt something sharp dig into her neck, heard something said over the sound of her music, but couldn't make it out.

Montessa tried to scream, kicking and fighting, but the hand over her hooded face pressed harder, and the steely sharpness pierced her skin. The trickle of blood running down her neck shocked her. The pain of the knife was so sharp, so sweet, so sudden and cold that she sucked in a breath as well as she could, reactively stiffening. Her legs wouldn't work anymore, but stuck out like the tiny wooden legs of dolls. The hand came off her mouth and wrapped itself around her ribcage, pinning her arms to her sides.

The voice again, right in her ear, "Move, and I'll kill you right here."

The blade pressed into her throat again, that same shock, the sheer surprise of being cut, of her skin being rent, of her blood, which was so precious, being wasted in such a careless way.

She was dragged backward, away from the road, away from help, away from the path that would lead her back to Renan.

Oh, thank goodness, she caught herself thinking, and it was a surprise. Then there was a great, ringing pain in her head, and she was relieved of thinking for a while.

CHAPTER TWO

ONTESSA AWOKE AND moaned. Renan's blows had been nearly unbearable this time. She blinked, but the room remained dark.

"Decided to wake up?" The voice was soft, surprisingly so. The words were spoken intimately like a lover would, but she didn't recognize the voice, except to say that it was strangely beautiful and foreign.

The hood was yanked off her head, and Montessa blinked in the dim light that came from a small lamp. Even that light was too much.

"I'm going to throw up," she said. A shadow suddenly swooped close, holding a large, plastic bowl in front of her face. She retched, twice. Montessa realized the stranger was holding her hair back from her face. "Thank you," she whispered when she was done. The bowl was emptied. The stranger mopped at her face with a damp baby wipe. She closed her eyes to keep out the light.

"I don't like filth. Don't mistake this for tenderness."

That soft voice again.

She nearly laughed. She felt her lips turn up despite herself.

"I won't."

Silence.

She felt the stranger perch beside her. She opened her eyes and stared at her feet. During the struggle, she seemed to have lost one of her shoes. She felt a vague sense of loss for it, but decided that mourning wouldn't do her any good. When had it ever?

"You think this is funny?" He didn't sound angry, just curious.

Montessa swallowed hard. Assessed. The headache made it feel as though her skull had split in half, but her mind was fairly clear. She was tied to a metal folding chair, bound at wrists and ankles, waist and shoulders. She couldn't get out if she tried. She glanced at the red stain on her shirt, blood from her throat. Escaping wasn't an option. Not now, anyway.

Her hair hung in her face, and she tossed it out of her eyes. Felt her skull scream. Grimaced.

"It isn't funny. It's . . . apt."

She felt him eying her. Felt the anxiety crawling under his skin like flames. Fire. Smoke. Steam.

"You don't act like most of the girls I take."

Montessa wasn't like most girls. She wanted to say it, but the room swam, and her stomach churned.

"Bowl," she said, and vomited, hard enough to choke and heave and cough. When she was finished, he wiped her face again, holding the tissue while she blew her nose. He gave her a glass of water and let her spit it out into the bowl. "Thank you."

"It's weird that you keep thanking me."

"I'm sorry."

"It's even stranger that you're apologizing."

She blinked up at him then, trying to make out

features, but all she saw was the glow of a cigarette in the dark. It moved and danced in a strange way, split into two and three. Fireflies. A swarm. She heard it in her head.

"Hey. Are you gonna puke again?"

She couldn't answer. The swarm of fireflies turned into something else. Flames. A city. On fire. Montessa whimpered, trying to pull away.

"Hey."

The bowl was in front of her, her hair pulled back again, but she couldn't take her eyes off the glow of his cigarette, of the flames running down the mountainside, of the open mouths of screaming people trapped inside buildings.

The stranger touched her, and she jerked away from his hands.

"Too hot," she said, but the words came out jumbled, slurred, and the fire ran across her body, charring her tender skin. Then, for the second time in as many hours, she fell unconscious.

Lu looked at the girl for a long time.

She didn't seem afraid of him or of being tied up. There had been an easy acceptance of her situation he wanted to ask her about. That he *would* ask her about. It was almost like she had seen into the core of him, seen what he was. Not The Man Who Had Taken Her, but the force of nature that was Lu.

He busied himself cleaning out the bowl. Pulling the girl's hair back and tying it with a rubber band, just in case. Checking to make sure the metal chair was firmly fastened in place so it didn't move, that she was breathing easily. He'd had one suffocate before while he was driving. What a shame. Such a loss. He'd cursed for days after that one, and had to find another right away to stuff food into the hunger. It happened much sooner than he had planned, of course. It had been dangerous, and close. Too close.

He climbed to the front of the semi, hopped behind the wheel, and started the truck.

Lu drove down the road, past the turn-off that the girl usually took to get to her house. A small thing, neat on the outside, thanks to her. He had watched her scrubbing and weeding and painting the trim. Saw her mowing the lawn in a pair of men's shorts and a white tank top. The boyfriend was never outside unless he was coming or going, a posse of men or women hanging around him. Lu wondered what the house looked like now. Destitute. Empty. Maybe it mourned for her in a way. Perhaps it knew she was leaving a hole that would never be filled. Wondered if it had cried when she left, knowing deep in its eaves she wouldn't return. Lu felt vaguely sorry for it, in a way, but not for long. You can't do what he does and give in to the weakness of sympathy.

He continued driving, leaving her house, and her boyfriend, and everything else that had any meaning to the girl, behind.

Montessa woke up somewhere in Idaho. She didn't know this at the time, of course. She just knew she was stiff and that she hurt from being tethered to the chair.

Her head felt a bit better, and the nausea was mostly gone, but her thirst became a problem. The hood made it hard to breathe. She tried to breathe shallowly, but she still inhaled the thin, dark fabric. It still fought its way into her mouth, wanting to coat her throat and airways with lint and thread and darkness.

Her breath started to come fast. She fought to slow it.

Montessa squirmed against the ropes uncomfortably. Testing. Feeling. The knots were tied. Her ankles were sore and raw. She still wore one shoe, which she kicked off, and wiggled her toes.

Better to lose both than to be constantly reminded of the one.

She had learned about loss early, learned about moving on as much as you could.

Her head swirled. Or maybe she was moving. She held her breath, listened, and heard the sound of revolving tires. Felt her body shift. She was definitely in a vehicle of some kind.

"Doing okay back there?" His voice was muffled but still strangely melodious.

"I need to use the restroom."

"Of course you do."

"And I really need a drink of water if you have one."

"Quite the demanding princess, aren't you?"

She didn't reply, just tipped her head back, willing her eyes to somehow see through the black fabric. Montessa swallowed hard, tried to keep the panic and despair down.

She felt the gravel underneath wheels, before they rumbled to a stop.

She heard her attacker clamber toward her, caught

her bottom lip with her teeth, and nipped it hard enough to draw blood.

Concentrate on that, Montessa, she told herself.

Montessa didn't want to wonder about who the man was and what he had in his hands. She had no desire to think if death was as peaceful as liars always said, or if it was gushing and bleeding and toned, bare legs drumming a sporadic rhythm on the ground as the last neurons fired off. She bit her lip again. Otherwise her screams would force themselves out of her belly and throat and she would scream both of them into oblivion.

"I'm going to untie your feet so you can use the camper toilet. I'll have my knife to your throat. Try anything and I'll kill you."

"You're going to kill me anyway, right? Why should this deter me?"

"If you want to be stuck like a pig while taking a piss, be my guest. It seems like a cheap way to go."

"I won't try anything. I just . . . please, hurry."

She felt his hands on her ankles, felt the tension of the ropes release. "Don't kick me."

"I already told you I won't."

He wrapped his hands around her waist, her shoulders. The ropes fell away. He yanked the hood off, pulled her awkwardly to her feet, and she groaned at her stiffness.

"My hands?"

"They stay tied. I'll pull your pants down for you."

`"I . . ."

"Relax. This isn't my thing. I certainly won't be getting off on it."

She thought she should be ashamed, that there

should be a stab of humiliation, but there wasn't. This wasn't any different than being a stripper, or any different than being used by Renan.

Using the restroom was a relief.

"Thank you," she said after he yanked her pants back up.

"You're exceptionally polite."

"For a kidnapped girl?"

"For anyone." He led her back to the chair, and she balked.

"I'm sorry. Could I stand for just a little bit longer? Even a minute or two?"

"Think you're in a position to ask for favors?"

"Mama taught me it never hurts to ask."

She looked him in the eyes then: dark brown, exotic, so dark that they almost seemed black. Pinpoints of light in them, fire at the corners. Her breath caught.

"I scare you."

It wasn't a question; it was a statement. He knew it. Knew it deep in his bones the way he knew he was a murderer. That he knew he was meant to be a lover to somebody, meant to go down in flames.

She swallowed hard. "Your eyes."

"What about them?"

His thoughts were plainly written on his face. He was waiting for her to discuss her fear. To tell him about his blackness, how he chills her.

For some reason, Montessa thought that he might've heard it before. A hundred times by now, at least. She saw his shoulders draw in, anger becoming prominent. Then, her kidnapper suddenly straightened and gritted his teeth together.

She heard his thoughts in her head. *Who has the knife, huh? Who is in charge here?*

"You are," she said, "but that wasn't what I was going to say. Your eyes have a fire inside of them. Like nothing I've ever seen. I just . . . that sounds silly." Sitting down, Montessa rearranged her arms behind her so they were as comfortable as her bound wrists could get. "You can tie me up again. I just wanted to move around a little bit, that's all, but I can see you're stressed and would like to get going."

Her kidnapper stared at her, stared into her eyes. Montessa knew her pupils didn't match, and her hair was matted, but he scrutinized her flaws intensely anyway. She thought he might've seen the dried blood on her head and down her throat, the angry wounds he'd caused. It didn't deter him, though, from binding her body too tightly to the chair and pulling the hood down roughly over her head again.

Montessa listened as he crawled back to the driver's seat, started the truck, and turned up the music. Way up. So he didn't have to hear her trying to calm her breathing in the back of the cab.

Night came.

He filled up at a gas station and grabbed some hot dogs and Cokes from inside. Then, he drove a good hour away from there before he let her use the bathroom again. The sigh of relief she breathed when he yanked the hood off, however, hurt him somehow. This made him angry. He tried hard to sound benevolent.

"I have some food. Hungry?"

"Yes, please."

"What will you give me for it?"

It was a cruel joke, but one that he often played. This was where they begged, offered him everything. Their body, their money, anything they had on them. This was when wedding rings came off and dignity peeled from their souls like their clothes from their bodies.

Lu laughed. It wasn't what he wanted, but the entertainment value was worth it. It's funny to think how little things like faith and honor and trust really mean when their bodies are on the line.

Montessa looked at him.

"For a gas station hot dog? I can sing. Would you like me to sing?"

Lu started. "Sing?"

"A song. Do you like songs?"

He didn't know what to say. He sat down on the little bed, beside her. "Nobody has offered me a song before."

"Do you want anything in particular, or should I choose?"

He unwrapped one of the hotdogs, took a bite, and watched her eyes follow it greedily. "You choose."

Lu watched as she closed her eyes, noticing one eyelid still discolored from earlier bruises. Of course her coward boyfriend would beat her. He turned his face away and took another bite. It didn't matter. None of this mattered.

She opened her mouth and began to sing. What he expected, he wasn't sure, but this soft and sweet and slow song sure wasn't it. The song reminded him of being a child, if being a child had been somewhat pleasant, which it wasn't.

He wanted to slap her mouth silent, wanted to watch her lip split. He wanted her to sing forever. He realized his fingers had curled into fists and were shaking, the hotdog squished in his hands.

"Stop it," he said, and she stopped. Just like that. A woman used to doing what she was told.

He threw her hotdog on the ground.

She looked at it, then up at him. "If it wasn't what you wanted, then you should have said so."

Her voice was calm.

Lu felt knocked off kilter. Shouldn't she be begging by now? "Nobody sings when they should be begging for their life."

She blinked her haunting eyes. "What should I have been doing, then?"

He snorted. "Most women offer me their body right away."

"I'm not most women."

He squatted down, picked up the hot dog, and peeled the foil back. "I know. Your mama told you that you were a little princess."

He held it out to her.

She took a bite, spoke with a full mouth. "No, I said that she told me I was special. There's a world of difference."

Then she ate, and the hot dog was gone faster than he would have expected. He had the feeling she would have licked the juice from his fingers if he would have let her. Again, Lu felt that feeling of something, something almost akin to sympathy. Again, he pushed it away.

"Thirsty?"

"Yes, please."

"I got a Coke."

"Do you have Diet?"

He started to laugh then, a sound that filled the dark cab, and it made her face hot and turned her stomach to ice at the same time.

"What, you're worried you're going to get fat? Put on a little weight while strapped to that chair?"

Her cheeks warmed. "I guess . . . you're right. What a silly thing to worry about. Got any chocolate while you're at it?"

She was joking. She was actually sitting there in restraints, trussed up in the back of a cab, and she was joking.

"Balls of brass," he said, and opened her drink. He slipped a straw in and held it for her. She drained the can quickly, so quickly, and he realized she probably was thirsty, that she had probably been thirsty after her night of dancing, that she had probably been looking forward to a long drink when she got home, but he had robbed her of that. For the first time, he felt something close to shame.

"Thank you," she said, and shifted uncomfortably on the chair.

Lu slammed the drink down. "Don't thank me. Stop thanking me. I'm not a nice guy."

"But I . . . what do you want me to say instead?"

He stood up. "Stop asking me that! Like you're some good, obedient pet or something. It's disgusting. You disgust me."

She silently swallowed and dropped her head, but

not before he saw the shine of tears in her eyes. Finally. She was going to act like a real victim.

"Want to know what's going to happen to you?" This was it: his speech. His Time to Tell. He reveled in explaining long, and slow, why each girl had been chosen, what their future held.

"You're going to kill me. With what? Your knife? You seem to like that knife."

Lu frowned. "I do like my knife, but I don't always use the knife, you see. There are other ways."

"Whatever you hit me with."

"The wrench. Sometimes, yes, but not usually."

"Why do you do it?"

He smiled. Dark. Predatory. "Because I want to."

Because I can. Because I'm a god in here. Nobody thinks less of me.

"They don't think that of you, anyway."

He snorted, not wanting to overthink why she said what she had. "Isn't this where you tell me that I don't have to do this?"

She shrugged as well as she could in the chair. "I don't think that would make a difference."

"You could try it."

She looked him in the eyes. "You don't have to do this."

"Yes, I do."

He tugged the hood back over her head, and imagined seeing her tears through the fabric, but of course it was impossible.

Lu didn't talk to her again until they were in Northern California.

"Hey. Desert Girl. Ever see the ocean?"

She started. She'd been asleep. "What?"

"The ocean. Ever see it?"

"No. I always wanted to, but never got out that way."

"Then I have a surprise for you." He grabbed her and dragged her roughly forward. She made a sound in her throat, something high and afraid and thrilling. Lu sat her in the passenger seat of his cab, used a padlock to fasten her bound wrists to the door handle, and pulled the hood from her head. The hood had left her hair mussed, and she rapidly blinked in the cloudy sunshine.

"Close your eyes," he said. She obeyed. He rolled down his window, the fresh air rolling in. She turned her face to it. "Smell that."

She smiled then, an innocent thing, a smile of pure joy. It hurt Lu's heart that he had to be the one to witness it. He wished it was anybody else. Could be anybody else.

"It smells just like I always imagined it would." Color came to her cheeks, just a little.

"You can open your eyes now."

Lu watched her from the corner of his eye. Large, liquid eyes sprang open, and the breath she took sounded too close, too intimate. Lu, who was used to seeing blood and viscera and the most hidden and secret of things, blushed and looked away.

"It's as beautiful as I had always hoped." Rocky. Blue. The water churned and pulsed far below them. Montessa pulled herself as far forward as her bound hands allowed. "Do you ever let people go out there?"

He looked at her. "What?"

"People. Girls. Your bodies. Do you ever . . . in the ocean?"

"Sometimes."

She watched the water with something exquisitely close to hope. "Would you possibly consider . . ."

"Disposing of you in the ocean?"

The color that came so recently to her face fled. "I don't like it when you put it that way."

"It is what it is, sweetheart."

"Why?" she asked, her eyes still on the sea. "Why do you have to make everything so horrible? Even if it has to be, why would you say it in such an awful way?"

He shrugged, leaned back in his seat, and put a cigarette into his mouth. "Why sugarcoat it? Doesn't change anything, does it?"

The cigarette burned.

"This just doesn't seem like you," she said.

He laughed around his cigarette. "You don't know anything about me."

"I know a lot more about you than you think." She turned to face him then, and her skin was pulled too tight across her face. "So how long do I have?"

He closed his eyes. "How come you always seem to know what I'm thinking?"

"How long?"

He sucked in hard, held the air in his lungs. Felt the burn from the inside out, but in a different way than he usually burned. "A few days, maybe. Until I get tired of you."

"Well, sure."

He opened one eye, studied her. "Why sound bitter all of a sudden?"

She turned to him, all skin and bones and rage in a tiny little package. "Who says you get to decide, huh? Maybe it'll be all over when I get tired of *you*."

His cigarette flared, erupted, fire spurting from the end and running up its length. He cursed and tossed it out his window. Opened his door and stamped it out. Cursed again. Stared at the girl bound in his passenger seat. She was staring right back.

Lu felt his heart do a strange thing.

It hurt. It opened. It beat.

CHAPTER THREE

THE MEATHEAD BOUNCER saw Montessa leave that night, but he didn't see where she went. Assumed she walked home if she didn't have a ride. She'd been walking home a lot lately.

"What's that supposed to mean?" Renan demanded. His voice was hot and dangerous, his eyes narrowed to slits. He took his aggression and turned it on high.

"Nothing. It just means that she's been walking home a lot lately. What's with the attitude, man?"

"You didn't see nobody pick her up or nothin'?"

"Not that I saw."

Renan ran his hand over his hair. "She'll be so sorry for this."

"Cool it. She could be in trouble. This doesn't seem like her."

Renan glared at the meathead. "And just how do you know anything about her, huh? Not supposed to talk to the girls, are you? Not supposed to talk to *my* girl."

The bouncer stepped forward. "Then maybe you should take care of your girl, huh? Keep an eye out for her."

"What was that?"

"You heard me."

Renan left with his anger burning slow. Didn't come home. Didn't get no food. Didn't call, nothing. She had a phone, right? Didn't pick it up. That's not what a good girl does.

That's what a girl does when she needs to be punished. He just had to find her first.

CHAPTER FOUR

IT SEEMED A shame to be so close to the sea and not to dabble in it just a little. There was nowhere Lu liked better. Sometimes he thought he'd been born of the sea, a Boy of Sorrows, and one day he'd simply walk back into the waves and disappear.

"Fitting," she said.

"Why is that?"

She stared at the ocean with a fierceness that belied her earlier good nature.

He saw long canines, guillotines, and axes in her eyes.

"You get rid of all of us, don't you? In pieces and parts. How many are found? How long does it take? You have this life of secrecy. And in the end, you think you'll just disappear and nobody will notice. It doesn't happen like that."

"It happens exactly like that."

"It doesn't. There's always somebody who will miss you. Somebody who will know you're gone. You think you can live on this Earth and not leave some kind of imprint?"

Had he been the laughing type, he would have laughed at this, but it didn't seem terribly funny. It just seemed terrible. "Who's going to miss you?" he asked. "Your mother? She's dead. Your father? You wish he was. Your boyfriend? Think he's gonna miss you?"

She leaned back against the seat. "Miss me? No. Look for me? That's something else altogether." She turned to face him. "He'll come looking. He probably already started. And when he does, you'd better be ready."

"I'm not afraid of him."

"You should be. I am."

Lu sighed. Hopped out of the cab, went around, and wrenched Montessa's door open. Her hands, still padlocked to the door handle, were yanked away, and she nearly fell out. Lu grabbed her wrists, looked deep into her eyes. "Are you going to scream?" he asked her.

She swallowed hard. "Are you going to kill me?"

"Not right now, no."

"Then I won't scream."

His skin was perfectly smooth, not a muscle moving. There was horror in such tranquility, in such lack of despair. He was raging inside, pacing inside of his brain with deft movements, but outside was that terrible placidity.

"I won't. I promise."

He nodded once, curtly, and unlocked her wrists from the door. They were still bound together, and he grabbed the rope with one hand. "Come on, then."

He dragged her down a craggy path, where she stepped on rocks and pebbles and pieces of sharp shell with her bare feet, but clamped her lips together. She wouldn't cry out. She'd take that pain deep inside of herself. Wrap her soul around it. Tether herself. He didn't slow down as he pulled her along behind him.

Anyone watching from far away would only see a young man with shiny black hair leading his girlfriend down to the water. Something sweet. Something playful. Montessa closed her eyes briefly. So few people see what's right in front of them: the beauty and magic and misery and sorrow. It's all lost.

"Keep up," he growled and yanked her closer to him.

She banged her knee against a large rock and yelped. Montessa bit her lip again and limped down to the beach behind him. The waves were white and frothy and furious. Not the cool, soothing waves that were shown on tropical beaches.

"They're angry," she said and tried not to notice when he watched her from the corner of his eye.

"That's a stupid thing to say."

Her ears burned. "Stupid to you or not, it doesn't make it any less true."

They watched the waves, heard the crashing, and noticed the sun coloring the clouds orange.

"I want to go in," Lu said, pulling on her bound hands again. "Let's go."

"I don't know how to swim," she said, and for the first time, her voice shook.

Lu nearly smiled. "You won't need to."

The water was shockingly cold around her ankles and knees. The salt stung the wounds on her bare feet, the scratches on her arms and legs, but at the same time . . .

"Why are you crying, girl?"

"My name is Montessa," she said, and that's all she could say. The water moved in and out, over her skin and around her legs, seeping into her soul. Tears fell down her face, mixing into the ocean, and Lu thought about how he had heard salt water healed everything. Sweat and tears and the sea. Maybe it was true.

He drew her farther out. The waves bumped around their knees and thighs. They both gasped at the cold around their waists and chests. The waves drew back, roared around their shoulders, and drew back again. Lu put his arm around Montessa's waist to keep her from falling.

"I always wanted to see the ocean," she said, and she was crying again, her wet hair falling into her eyes and spilling over his hands.

"I'm sorry it's with me," Lu told her, and realized it was the first time he had ever apologized to a victim, and his blood burned, boiled, and the water churned around them.

"Too hot," Montessa gasped out, spitting water from her mouth. Lu took a deep breath, tried to control his rage, tried to cool the water before it gave them blisters, tortured even more by the heavy salt.

"Let's go," he said roughly, and she followed, wiping her eyes awkwardly on her wet shoulder, her clothes dripping and salt baptizing her body.

"Thank you," she said quietly when they reached the cab. Her clothes were wet, but not dripping. She climbed in obediently, moved to the back, and sat in her chair without fighting. "May I please keep my hands in front of me this time? It really hurts to have them tied behind me." Lu paused. "I won't do anything," Montessa said. She smiled, and it was full of sadness so bright that Lu nearly bared his teeth at it. "You probably figured it out by now. I'm not the type of person who does . . . anything." She looked away, blinking her eyes again.

Lu had seen enough salt for the time being.

He let her bound hands rest in her lap, tied her firmly to her chair. "Go to sleep," he said and slid into the driver's seat.

He noticed the black hood lying between the door and the seat. He stuffed it into the jockey box, shifted into gear, and started to drive.

CHAPTER FIVE

"**T**HIS GUY?**"** Lu said.

"Renan."

"Yeah. Him. Why are you guys together, anyway? He's obviously a complete tool."

Montessa stayed silent. This was where she was supposed to defend Renan. Tell her kidnapper she was in love, that he didn't know her boyfriend, that he couldn't make judgments on the wonderful man that she committed her life to.

"Hey. Girl."

"I told you it's Montessa. Why don't you tell me your name?"

"I don't want to."

"It's Lu."

"How did you know that?"

She looked out of the window. He'd let her into the front of the cab, shackled her to the door handle again. It was dark. The seat was soft and comfortable and felt like luxury. She had told Lu as much. He said he was frightened that such small things made her happy. She must be awfully used to being miserable, he said, if such tiny things meant so much.

"There's a lot of energy to you, Lu. Built up under

your skin. Behind your eyes. One day, you're just going to explode."

She turned to him, studied his profile in the light of the oncoming traffic. He looked straight ahead, but his eyes smoldered in a way that made her stomach lurch. His lips moved slightly. A tic. Everything sewn tightly together, kept under control. A tiny muscle spasm in his lips, that was all.

"You think so?" he asked, and was surprised to find that he cared, maybe just a bit. He wanted to find out what this woman thought of him, what she could see. Or See. Whatever it was.

"I think so. That's why you kill, isn't it? To release the anger? The steam?"

He continued to not look at her. She continued to breathe in air without a hood, to sit on a chair that wasn't metal, to be unbound except for her wrists and ankles.

As she had said: luxury.

"My first kill . . . " he started to say. He swigged a drink of Coke. Stopped speaking. Checked the side mirrors instead.

"Your first kill?" she prompted.

He faced her then, and the look he wore was the look of two faces in constant battle with each other. One of snarling hate, a fierceness that made Montessa want to close her eyes, to turn her throat away from his canines. The other: that was the other Lu. A sad, miserable boy trapped inside a man's body. Somebody who cried while he sliced seams in suits of flesh. Somebody who ran bloodied hands through his dark hair, spiking it even more than usual.

"Lu. And Lu. Lulu," she said, and was surprised

when he laughed. It was a bitter sound, the sound of comfrey petals and bryony roots, things mixed together that shouldn't be, and Montessa's stomach lurched.

"You know all about me, don't you, Crazy Girl? I bet they called you a witch growing up. I bet they still do. Your boyfriend especially, before he beats you? During? While making love?"

She blinked her too-pale eyes. Her lips had been curving upward slightly, but the smile curled down into a frown. She looked out of the window again.

Lu felt like cursing, suddenly. Like grabbing her hair, leaning back, and yanking. Pulling it out by the roots, seeing if it really was that dark, that soft. Making her scream until her head blew, throwing blood against the windows of the cab.

Did her boyfriend do that to her, he wondered?

It made him sick. It made him no better. And Lu desperately wanted to be better than that piece of trash.

"We don't make love," she said. Her voice was low. There was a hollowness, a sadness to it he didn't expect. It made Lu cold inside, and he wasn't a man used to being cold. He ran hot. Ran *just* on this side of explosive rage. His blood boiled all the time, and sometimes it came out through his fists, his hands, the lick of his knife.

He didn't like this, the change. He wanted to wrap something warm around himself. *Her arms, her hair,* he thought briefly. This startled him. He gasped.

"Making love is something different," Montessa continued. "There's no love there. Not for either of us. I don't think there ever was."

"Then why do you stay? You've been with him for a long time."

"You've been watching me for a long time."

He shrugged. "Among others. I watch all of you. I want to know who I'm taking."

She wanted to ask him about it, but that would come later—if there was a later. She found she didn't care. She found that the past and now and later all rolled together into one big ball of . . . something. Regret? Apathy. She liked apathy better than regret anyway.

"He was somewhere to be, I guess. A warm body. And he said he loved me, at first."

"Did he?"

"I don't think so, but it didn't matter. The words are nice, even if there isn't any intent behind them. I guess."

Lu's face changed again, becoming dark. His breath sounded like the howl of dead things.

Montessa smiled at him, a real smile, and Lu was struck in the heart by the force of it. The beauty. A blade of sincerity. He couldn't breathe.

"You're upset for me, Lulu. Aren't you." It wasn't a question. It was her knowledge, the Things She Knew, and Lu didn't have anything to say. "That's . . . sweet. That means something. Thank you."

She was still smiling, but a tear ran down her face, and then another. Silently. Traitorous. Neither of them had even known they were there. The tears and the smile and her dirty, matted hair . . . juxtaposition. The most exquisite of miseries. Lu caught his breath again. It burned inside his lungs, charred the tender tissues there.

Montessa laughed, and it hurt. Cut. It was a slicing sound, mirth and desolation and a special type of wretchedness that only beautiful, dying women can experience.

"Do you realize," she said, "that you might be the only person in this entire world who even remotely cares about me. You're angry for me, for the waste of my life. And you're going to kill me. Do you realize how sick that is? How sad?"

Tears illuminated her eyes this time, making their presence fully known, and it was a horrifying sight. Lu had wanted tears. Hoped for them. Prayed for them, sometimes, and the irony of that wasn't lost on him. But these tears felt wrong to him. He wanted to lick them off her face with his tongue, taste if they were as bitter as they seemed. For the first time, perhaps, he didn't want to watch the weeping of a woman.

"If you're the one that cares the most," she whispered, "then what kind of person am I? To be so unlovable?"

He could say something now, something to make it better, which he desperately wanted to do for some reason. He could say that Renan was obviously a jerk, that people make mistakes, especially in love. That she wasn't unlovable. After all, didn't the men and women at the strip club adore her? Get extra excited whenever *Ruby* undulated onto the stage? Didn't she have a magic in her hips and lips that nobody else could match?

That wasn't what he wanted to say. It wouldn't help; it would only hurt. But he needed to say something. Any small thing. Offer what comfort he could even if it was only to explore this unusual feeling of not wanting to hurt, crush, kill. If just for a second.

"I'll make it quick," he promised her, and the earnestness in his voice terrified him. He meant it. He'd bleed her out quickly, releasing her to the universe at the very first instead of hearing her shriek at every slit, every cut, every pound on her tender flesh. Maybe he wouldn't even play as much afterward. Maybe he would release her, and it would be a kindness, perhaps his first, and then he . . . then what? "And I'll take your body to the sea."

She laughed, and Lu cringed, smarting. He never offered things. To have it rejected, well, it stung. More than he would have thought, actually.

"Thank you, my Lulu. I appreciate what you're saying. How much it took you to do it. But it doesn't matter." She turned her face to the window and closed her eyes against her reflection. "It just doesn't matter."

Lu bit the inside of his cheek. Let her cry. Maybe she deserved it after all. That release. You can't fault a nearly-murdered woman for crying. It's a natural part of the process.

A few more days. A few more states. A few more conversations, and then he'd kill her. She'd be grateful for it, in a way, he was sure of it. But first he'd tell her about his first kill. It would be a gift to her. Something for her to think about while the light faded from her eyes.

And, perhaps, he could give her one more gift, too. Giving didn't come naturally to Lu. It was a new feeling, stretching wings that were clumsy and ill-fitting and misshapen, but there was a delicious burn to it at the same time. Working muscles that were shrieking out for it.

Yes. A gift for the girl. For Montessa. He'd think on it while he drove. He'd think quite hard.

CHAPTER SIX

WANNA TAKE A walk?" Lu asked. He was tired of driving. His back ached, and his legs were cramped, and his head was full of cotton or bees or bloodlust. Sometimes it was difficult to tell which. Montessa hesitated. Lu tossed her a look. "What? I thought you'd be all over getting out and stretching your legs."

She swallowed hard. "Is this a killing sort of walk?"

Lu frowned. He didn't know why. He felt his lips curl and turn and stretch, felt his eyebrows furrow and his eyes spark. He was slightly offended. A killing sort of walk, indeed.

"Nah, lady. It's just a walk. A normal, everyday kind of walk."

"Call me Montessa," she said, and stared out of the window again.

He pulled over on the shoulder, next to a group of trees. Thick. Leafy. Perfect cover. Wonderfully remote-feeling. The type of place where, yes, he would gladly go on a killing walk. But that made his newly-beating heart heavy somehow.

"I will kill you, you know. Just not now."

"I know." Her voice, it had that ghostly sound

again. Hopeless. Airy. Leaves and trees and dried twigs scratching against her larynx.

"You didn't seem too concerned about dying earlier," he said, accusingly. The emotion of that made him frown again, deeper. He lit a cigarette to cover the shaking of his hands, of his thoughts. She didn't answer. He hopped out of the cab, went around, let her out. They both used the bathroom, and then he nodded. "Go on. You can walk in front."

She blinked, and he realized how pale she was. How filthy her hair and body were. Normally he would have washed her down by now with a washrag while she begged and screamed and prayed, but that seemed invasive somehow, like he should ask her permission. That wasn't right. That wasn't how this game was played.

"You're not going to hold on to me?"

"I will if you want me to. I just figured . . . "

"No, you figured right. Thank you."

"Run, and I'll kill you."

"I know. You don't have to keep saying it, Lulu. It's insulting at this point." So she walked ahead of him, gingerly, and he realized she was barefoot, the pads of her feet still cut and bleeding from the rocky beach. The tops and sides were being scraped now by roots and pine needles, but she didn't seem to care. "The trees smell so good," she said and reached out with her bound hands to touch the pine needles. She sniffed one, bit into it. The bitter taste flooded her mouth, reminding her of when she was a little girl. Why, Montessa didn't know. She didn't remember pines. She only remembered dead Mama and sweaty Father's fists and the boys down the street who did things to motherless little girls.

She spit the pine needle out. Filled her mouth with saliva and spit that out, too.

Lu watched her, saw the way her eyes turned colors they shouldn't be able to. Watched her face go taut and hard and frightening in a way. Her hair began to move of its own accord, blown by a fierce wind he couldn't feel, and he knew Something Big was happening. Something dangerous.

"Hey," he said, and when she turned to face him, her eyes were very far away. Frosted over like icy ponds. She held her bound hands in front of her and he saw that they were raw, bloodied. Sticky burns around her wrists that would scar, if she lived that long. And of course she wouldn't live that long. She was a woman already dead, only her body hadn't caught up with her soul yet. "Montessa," he said softly, and her name filled his mouth like the best of his mother's cooking, like a smooth stone, something like hope. "Montessa," he said again, and her eyes thawed. Refocused. Her hair stopped blowing in the Wind-That-Wasn't and settled around her thin shoulders again.

"I'm sorry," she said, and staggered. He grabbed her automatically by the ropes around her wrists, saw them dig into the wet, oozing wound. The body liquid. Pus and despair produced by pain. He cursed and put his arm around her shoulders.

"Don't collapse on me. I don't feel like hauling you back to the cab."

"I'm sorry," she repeated, and the strength in her body went. Lu guided her to the ground. Without him, she would have gone down like a gunshot victim.

"Tired? Hungry?"

"I just need a second."

"Demanding little princess."

Lu squatted beside her, pulled the knife out of its sheath. Reflected it in the light, back and forth. Back and forth.

"Trying to scare me, Lu?"

He didn't like this weak voice. It didn't sound like her, like the girl he thought he knew.

"Are you scared?"

He didn't like his voice either. Angry. Maybe a touch of hurt under it all.

He growled.

Montessa smiled at him briefly. Barely. The tiniest of smiles. The smallest curve of her split and dried lips.

"So angry. Nuclear Lulu. I told you that one day you're going to blow."

"What happened back there?"

"Mama always said I was special." She closed her eyes, looking perfectly and beautifully and horrifyingly dead. Lu held the knife far above her, tracing it over her veins and cheekbones. He mentally took it to her hair, removed her eyes.

Loss. He tasted it.

He pressed the blade against the pad of his index finger. So sweet. So sharp. His blood filled the line that it left, dripped onto the ground, which devoured it hungrily.

"My dad tried to kill me with this knife," he said. He studied the red on it, wiped it clean on his cargo shorts. "When he found out what I was. What I could do. He called me a demon."

Montessa opened her eyes, watched him, felt the importance in what he was saying. Recognized that he was sharing, and it hurt, and was frightening, and he was more than likely to kill her now than ever. Share, and then murder. Let yourself be vulnerable, and then erase all proof that such a thing ever happened.

She hoped that when she went, it would be like releasing her soul to the butterflies. She wished for it fervently.

Lu stared at her. He grinned, and his teeth looked very sharp.

"He would have called you a demon, too. A devil girl. He grew up in China and still has some of the old ideas." He studied his knife again. "I wish he had just said I was special, like your mama told you."

Her breathing had been fast, frantic, pushed up-tempo by fear and thoughts of her father and her jagged anticipation of Lu's dagger. She tried to slow it. Thought of Lu as a young boy, as a teenager, as a person who was considered evil by his father.

"My father thought I was evil, too," she said, and swallowed the words.

"Yeah? Did he call the shaman? The priest? Try to exorcise the devil out of you?"

"He tried everything."

Lu sighed. "So did my dad. None of it worked. I was still . . . me."

"There's nothing wrong with you being you."

He bared his teeth at her. Maybe it was supposed to be a smile. Neither one of them was quite sure.

"You don't know anything about me, Devil Girl."

She closed her eyes again, still weak. "I know that you're you. And that's enough. Your daddy couldn't ask for more than that."

He watched her. He touched his tongue to the steel

of the dagger. He'd licked it clean before, so many times. Used it to butcher. Used it to eat meals. Used it to dig in the dirt a few times, although he was afraid it would damage the blade, the shining oracle that he kept so nice and sharp.

"How many people have the knife that somebody tried to kill them with?" he asked her, and realized that he really cared. This knife, it was supposed to be an ugly thing. A thing of horror, but he had taken it from his father's clenched fist and done something else with it. Made it work for him. Made it serve him. He stole the terror away from it by inflicting that terror on everybody else who saw it.

The other women. Montessa.

She'd never be just another girl, now.

He remembered her name, always would, he thought, and he seldom remembered names. They just weren't important.

"This knife," he said, and held it out so she could see it. "This knife, it's important. Important in a way that most things aren't important. Does that make sense?"

"You reclaimed it," she said, and the word sounded just right. Reclaimed. Taken back. Made his own.

"Yes," Lu said, and his voice was proud. "I did."

Her eyes were still closed, her voice tired. "Is that why you like it so much? To get back at your father? To show him that he didn't beat you?"

Lu scratched at his chin. Looked at the knife again and put it away. He studied his hands, which were long and elegant. Piano hands, his mother had said, but he had no talent with the piano. Or the violin. Or tailoring tuxedos, which was what his father did. But murder?

Peeling skin, neatly and smoothly? Making the cuts neat and tidy, perfect in every way? That was a talent he did possess. Something he could share with the world. Something he chose to.

"I don't need to show him anything, anymore."

"Why is that?" Her voice sounded dreamy. Lu realized she was nearly asleep, and that wouldn't do. Stay too long in one spot and somebody will inevitably stumble upon them. Wonder why the brunette was tied up. People tend to frown on bound women out in the wilderness. "I won't fall asleep," she reassured him. "I'll get up in just a minute for you. But the sky, it feels so good. The air. The trees. It isn't like home at all. And that's a good thing." She sighed, a sound like contentment, but it couldn't be. Not trussed up here in the forest with the man who was going to murder her. Lu frowned. "Stop worrying, Nuclear Lulu. Tell me about why you don't have to prove anything to your dad anymore."

He shrugged. "He's dead. Gone. Can't hurt nobody no more."

"I'm sorry," she said. She opened her eyes, and he saw sincerity in them.

His smile, it was wolfish. His smile, it was sly. "Don't be sorry. I'm not sorry. I'm happy. Delighted, almost. It was the best thing that ever happened to me. Dad was my first kill."

Her gaze sharpened, clarified, and something moved in her eyes then. Something with scales. Something that made him suck his breath in. His stomach twisted in the most painful and delicious of ways.

"You killed your father," she said, and struggled to

sit up. He let her do it herself, not wanting to pull on her bloodied wrists again. When she managed to sit, she put her face uncomfortably close to his. "Tell me, Lu. Tell me all about it. Please? Please."

There wasn't anything he wanted to do more. "We have a long drive ahead of us. Let's go back to the truck and get started. Then I'll tell you all about it."

She picked her way back gingerly. He didn't say anything else until the engine roared and made the angry sounds that Lu had made in his throat when his father had lunged at him with the knife. The growl turned into something else, something primal and loud and unstoppable. A force of nature. A wildfire. He had wrenched the knife from the old man's hand, making the handle white-hot, and the wrinkled skin had flamed and smoked and charred while the knife was thrust up, under his rib cage, and it was the most terrifying and exhilarating moment in Lu's young life.

"I was free," he said, and Montessa watched him with her quiet eyes. Lu realized that he had said "I was free" without any other preface. Maybe she needed to hear the entire story first, but he started with the part that *mattered* before anything else. And being free, that's what mattered. More than anything. Most of all.

"I was free," he said again, and nodded, because that was exactly right. Then he grinned at her, a breathtakingly beautiful grin, although he didn't know this, of course.

But Montessa's throat closed, and her heart shuddered in her chest at the easiness, at the joy, at the satisfaction of that grin. And that smile, those white teeth. That was the beginning of this for her.

That was the second that she decided maybe she wanted to live after all.

CHAPTER SEVEN

RENAN HAD FAVORS. Lots of them. Things owed to him since before the dawn of time, it seemed, and this was the perfect time to call them all in.

Monty had been gone for over a week now. A week. No calls. Nothing. And that wasn't right, wasn't what a woman was supposed to do for her man. He found himself seeking comfort wherever he could find it, cursing her name with each bump, each hit, each woman. She was selfish, making him worry. Running off and passing her little whorish self around to any panting dog that looked at her. Laughing at him, he knew it. He just knew.

So he called in his favors. Had sets of eyes looking for her everywhere. If she used her credit card, if she showed up on any newsfeed, if she stuck her head out anywhere in the country, he'd find her. He'd drag her back, screaming, if he had to. Then he'd make her pay. Oh, he'd enjoy that part. Making her pay was like nothing else on Earth. It was like hearing the angels sing.

CHAPTER EIGHT

MONTESSA WAS ENTHRALLED. She watched Lu's mouth while he spoke, watched the way he used his hands, the way his emotions changed his face according to where he was in the story.

He talked about his dad's abuse, about the way he hid in his closet as a little boy. The way they took him to rituals and the shamans beat their drums and how he ate the special foods meant to cleanse the soul and body. Lu had set the shaman aflame the last time his parents took him. She had been put out quickly. Maimed but not murdered. Scarred but alive.

"So not my first kill, but almost," he said, and the way his eyes twinkled, it was like something out of a fairytale.

"Tell me how it felt to kill your father," Montessa urged, and even though he had already told her, he told her again. And again, when she asked for it a third time. She was a child with a favorite bedtime story. Tell me again, please. Again. More and more and more.

"The way his bones cracked, it was like nothing I'd ever imagined," he said. His voice, the excitement, it made her blood run faster through her veins, screaming through arteries like a rollercoaster. "The smell of his clothes as they burned. The heat. I watched his sparse hair burn right off his head, and it was . . . oh, Montessa, it was something special."

She liked the way he said her name. She liked it very much.

"Ever feel like you have a calling?" he asked. "Something you're really good at? That it was made for you to do, and you'll never be happy unless you're doing it?"

"That's how you feel? That you were meant to kill your father?"

"Absolutely. Nothing ever felt so right. It was almost like being a priest: taking the evil out of the world. I was doing the universe this big favor, right? It was almost holy."

She wanted to ask if it felt like that with the other girls, if it was holy, as well. Were they being sacrificed on the altar of some god? Was he communing with a type of spirit as he slit throats?

She was almost jealous.

"When you kill me," she said, and noticed that Lu blinked furiously, as if startled, "will you remember me? Maybe not as fondly as you remember your father's death, of course, but will I . . . " She didn't know how to finish. Would she mean something to him? Fulfill him in some way? Could he sup on her soul for a little while, until he felt the need to take another woman, another life, and she became just another body in a line of bodies? "Never mind," she said. "I don't really want to know."

He was quiet. Thoughtful. When he spoke, his voice was low and melodious, and she remembered how smooth and calm it had been when she first heard it through the hood.

"I told you I'd dispose of you in the sea."

Her smile, it was sunny. Full of radiance and joy and peace.

"Thank you," she said, because she knew what he was saying.

"You're welcome," he answered, and blushed a bit on his high cheekbones, because he knew what she had been asking.

The silence in the cab was companionable. Soft and sweet. He wanted to reach out and hold her hand, run his fingertips against her fragile knuckles, but her hands were still shackled to the door handle, out of his reach.

That was when Lu realized he was going to let her go.

CHAPTER NINE

H**IS HEART HURT** in a strange new way. Felt too tight, like it was bound and everything in him screamed to take his knife to the knotted tissue and whatever iron band had wrapped around it. Release it. Take away the hurt. Take away this pain. Lu didn't like it, not at all.

It came from letting the girl go. He knew this. When she left, she'd go directly to the police and tell them all about the young Asian man, early 20s, surprisingly muscled and wiry, maybe 130 pounds. 150? He usually wore a T-shirt. A dirty denim jacket when things got cold. Jeans and sneakers. Oh, yes, and he had a knife—long, shiny, very clean and very sharp knife. He murdered his father with that knife. He drives a semi. His name is Lu. He's killed several other girls. When you find him, it should be the death penalty all the way, please. He hit me in the head with a wrench. It hurt so terribly, so terribly that I threw up, over and over and over. It's a miracle I got away.

He'd be dead before the police organized their search. Dead before they found him, threw him to the ground, and cuffed him. He wasn't going to live his life in a box. Wasn't going to relive his precious kills for them, so some strange families could have *closure*. He didn't care about their closure. He'd give himself to the sea first.

"What are you thinking about, Lu?" she asked him.

"Shut up and go to sleep."

He felt her hurt, a tangible thing. It rested on his tongue like snowflakes, like cocaine, bitter and worn and familiar. She was so used to hurting that she practically wrapped it around herself like a blanket. A soft, thin protection. The most ineffective of armors.

He sighed.

"I have to drop my load off tomorrow. Empty the truck. I'm trying to figure out what to do with you first, okay?"

"What do you usually do with your girls?"

A beat. A pregnant pause, as they said in books. A time where the air in the cab grew heavy and dark and expectant and full of responsibility. He didn't want the responsibility. Didn't need it. He wanted to kick the door open, roll out onto the moving ground beneath him, and pelt down the road away from her. She knew what he did. He knew she knew. She wanted to hear him say it, to be beaten down by his words. So he said them.

"Kill them."

"Oh."

"You asked."

"I did."

She turned her face to the window, and Lu cursed. Cursed louder and hit the steering wheel. "Dammit, Montessa, enough of that!"

She turned back, her face white, and her mouth dropped open. He saw it, saw the blood running from the corners of her mouth, saw her eyes swollen shut and the bruises that colored and puffed her face. Saw how many times hands had been put on her, and that she expected the same from him.

He'd already done so.

He blinked, and the gore was gone. She was just terrified. Terrified and whole, her cuts and wounds having healed while they had been together, for the most part.

His heart twisted again.

"You accept too much, do you understand me? Your mama said you were special. So be special. Enough of this beaten animal act all of the time."

She pulled away from him, made herself into a small ball near the window, and that was all he needed. And the perfect opportunity.

He pulled the truck over, too fast, and the brakes hissed and puffed and threw up gravel like sheets of water.

"Lu? No!"

He reached over her, so close that he could smell her sweat and fear and something that tasted like sorrow, and unlocked the padlock. He grabbed her bound hands and pulled her roughly between the seats.

"Lu! Lu, please! I don't want to die!"

He pulled her close to him, her hands up in the air, shaking them.

"Is that true?" he asked.

Her breath came heavy and fast. Her muscles were rigid, her too-pale eyes wide and frightened, and at the same time, smoldering with something darker.

Horror? No. Fury.

Lu nearly smiled, but caught himself in time.

"Huh, girl? Is it true? Do you want to live?"

She couldn't speak, but nodded. Her face was so close to his that she could lift her chin and bite deeply into his bottom lip, if she wished. Tear it and spit the blood back at him. He almost hoped that she would. Teach him a lesson. Make him sorry. Hurt him so good.

She blinked, and he was satisfied to see there weren't any tears there.

He threw her onto the bed built into the corner.

"If you want to live, then act like it."

He felt the set of his face, the granite under his skin, as he climbed back into his seat and started the truck. A breeze flew around the cab, a storm, a tornado of ill feeling, and he heard the chair fall over and slide around in the back. Knew that Montessa was raging inside. If he was lucky enough, she'd go apocalyptic and incinerate them all, but she wasn't at that point, not yet. Perhaps she never would be. But, oh, how he hoped so.

He'd sleep in the driver's seat tonight. Let her have the back. Free to roam, free access to his tool box. She'd cut the ropes around her wrists, and then what? Stab him in the neck? Possibly. Try to creep out without his noticing? He wouldn't sleep a wink, he knew it, but he wouldn't try to stop her. Let her go. Let her be free. She'll go back to whatever life she would go back to. Her boyfriend would probably kill her. It seemed a shame that he would get to do so and Lu wouldn't. Lu would have made it kind. Appreciated it. Filed it away in his mind of Beautiful Kills. Remembered her fondly, both alive and as a corpse.

He wanted her in a way that loser wasn't even capable of.

He realized his jaw ached from clenching too hard. He tried to relax, tried to focus on the road, on the whistling of the Montessa-created storm around his ears. Think of the here and now. The imminent. Don't spend any time wondering how soft her hair would be when it was freshly washed and free of sticky blood. He realized, with surprise, for the first time he would miss somebody.

He nearly ran off the road, righted the truck quickly. Sucked in a breath and held it.

It was true. He was going to miss her.

CHAPTER TEN

HER HAIR SWIRLED around her, and her breaths came in gasping almost-sobs of rage that she tried to rein in. The pressure behind her eyes, in her head and chest pushed out, nearly exploding from behind her eyes and teeth. If she didn't hold back, she'd blow the truck apart, she could feel it. Kill herself and Lu and there wouldn't be anything to find, just tiny bits of rubble and detritus carried on the wind.

She had to calm down. Breathe. Breathe, breathe, breathe.

Montessa held her hands to her face, her wrists bloodied and sore and raw. With her eyes covered, things seemed less pressing. She was here. She was safe. He had put her here to let her escape. She knew this and appreciated it on a level, too, of course. Of course she did. But at the same time . . .

I'm tired of being tossed away.

Abandoned by her mother. Used up until her body and soul ground into little bits by her father or at least the man that she had been trained to think of as her father. Used and left by her cousins. The neighbors. Everybody.

Renan hadn't trashed her. He was frightening and

abusive, and he scared her so deeply that her guts pooled in her bowels, that she tasted vomit whenever he leaned in to bite or kiss her, she never knew which one. But he hadn't left. He threatened to kill her if she walked out on him. That's the opposite of leaving, isn't it?

It isn't love. Of course it isn't love, and Montessa had never deluded herself into believing love entered into the equation with Renan. Still, he wanted her around. To control, certainly. To beat on and break. But to keep. Regardless of the consequences.

Being kept was the opposite of being abandoned, and Montessa had walked down enough dirt roads, wiping the blood from her mouth with the back of her hand, to know she wanted to stay. Be kept. It wasn't so much to ask. Nothing to ask, really.

"Lu isn't Renan," she said aloud, and this calmed her a little. Lu's motivations were as lofty as a man like Lu's motivations could be. In fact, it was probably killing him inside to let her loose like this. She could peek inside and feel his emotions, take them into her own soul, but she was already too conflicted. She couldn't handle any more.

She curled up into a ball, wrapping her arms around herself and keeping her face covered.

Breathe, Montessa. Breathe. He wants you to go, and it's a gift. Take it as the favor he's offering. This doesn't mean you're trash.

It means you're special.

She'd seen enough of Lu's emotion to understand his confusion regarding her. Montessa knew Lu never wanted to let a girl go before. She knew that he didn't understand his desire to have her live. If he murdered her, slid his blade along her spine, tasted her arterial blood and tears, then he'd have her forever in a way. But this was different, and Montessa knew Lu didn't feel comfortable around anything different.

She scared him to death. And he scared her, but not in the way he thought. Not in the usual way a killer panics his victim.

Montessa bit her lip, concentrated on her breathing, calmed the wind down around her, and chose to enjoy the comfort of the soft bed built into the side of the cab. She thought of all the nights Lu must have slept here, how he'd lie on his back and stare at the ceiling, or curled on his side like she was doing. The bed was narrow but could hold two if they molded into each other's bodies while they slept. If they were close.

Hours. Hours of driving. She dozed, in and out of consciousness. Found an X-acto knife in Lu's toolbox and worked at the rope around her wrists. He heard her. She knew he heard her. He didn't say anything, and she didn't either. She wondered briefly if this was what marriage was like thirty years down the road. Being completely aware of each other but letting it all slide.

The filthy piece of rope fell to the ground, and Montessa flexed her hands, her wrists. Touched her tongue to the raw places, felt the burn and the hurt. She slipped the X-acto knife into the back pocket of her jeans and sat on the edge of the bed.

The truck slowed, pulled over. The engine turned off, and she heard Lu fidget around in his seat before feigning sleep. She waited until his breathing became slow and even, a courtesy on her part. Lu wouldn't sleep tonight. His head was too full of turmoil and voracious black teeth, of razor blades and loss. But he was trying. Bless the boy, he was trying.

She crept up between the seats. Saw the moonlight and the way it fell on Lu's quiet face, his beautifully curved eyes. So much torment beneath the surface, but looking at him now, he seemed placid. He was in a place of peace; if only there was such a place for Montessa.

She took the can of Coke from the console, unlocked the door to the passenger side. Stole one last glance at her Nuclear Lulu and slipped outside.

Morning came, and Lu cursed it, just like he cursed everything else. He sighed, stiff from sitting in the driver's seat, and stirred. Time to get up, time to get it all going. He'd had a good run. A good time, even. But it was time for it to end.

He'd peeked at Montessa from under his lashes last night as she'd stolen from the cab. Saw her take the drink and nearly smiled, but then felt it drop away. She had unlocked the door, and then looked at him one last time. He had stilled his breath, forced himself to lie quietly in the seat, when that wasn't what he wanted to do at all.

He wanted to leap to his feet, to grab her by her bloodied (thanks to him) wrists and tell her that it wouldn't be so bad, really, if she stayed. He'd kill her or not kill her, whatever she wanted. Knives or no knives. Guns or no guns. He'd do anything if she'd just agree to . . . what? Live in a semi with him until they both went down in flames?

Shame.

The piercing recognition that he had nothing to offer her. That a life with him would be worse than a life with her selfish boyfriend. Well, that stayed his hand and turned his body to stone. He let her go, watched her jump out of the cab, and mostly close the door behind her quietly.

He didn't want to move this morning. There was no reason to really. He could wait until the police came and bustled him away. Maybe it wouldn't be that bad. Maybe life in a cell before they fried him wouldn't be as horrible as he thought.

He was lying to himself, and Lu wasn't a liar. He sat up fully, sighed, and ran his fingers through his hair. Everybody dies. Might as well get to gettin' to it. There really wasn't a reason to stick around anymore, anyway.

He kicked open the cab door, dropped to the ground, turned his face toward the sun, and blinked.

"Hey."

He spun around and saw Montessa sitting on the ground, her back to one of the massive tires. She looked weary and filthy, and her lips and eyes were so full and big and beautiful.

"What are you doing here?" His voice sounded differently than he meant it to. Almost harsh. Almost angry.

Montessa flinched, but then she stood up slowly. "Tell me why you're letting me go."

Lu started. "What a stupid question! Why would you ask that? If a killer lets you go, then you go. You run. Why aren't you running?"

She took a step closer to him. Another. Lu noticed

vaguely that the Coke can was wedged under the tire, that it would be crushed when he pulled forward. What a random thought, and he wondered about it, but realized his brain was finding small things to focus on. It couldn't handle the big things, like Montessa standing in front of him, reaching out to grip his T-shirt in her small hands.

"Lu. Tell me. Why are you letting me go?"

"Leaving that can there is littering, you know. There are laws against it."

She laughed then, and he realized how bizarre his words must seem, but there *were* laws, and he wasn't going to get caught by some Woodsy Owl do-gooder over something so stupid.

"I'll pick it up if you tell me why."

He grabbed the hand clutching his shirt, and she hissed. He kept his grip there, felt the throbbing rawness of her wrist under his fingers.

"Stop asking like it's important."

"It is important."

"It isn't. It's just a random thing. No reason."

"You're planning to kill yourself today before I turn you into the cops."

"How did you . . . ?"

"You know how."

He glared at her then, his eyes fiery and flaming and full of fury and helplessness. "Then see why I let you go. Do it. Save me the aggravation."

She studied him, the thin scar by his eye, the neat, blunt fingernails on his hands. The way his chest heaved under his shirt. He could barely catch his breath.

She swallowed hard. "Please. Just tell me. If you

don't want me to stay, then I'll go. I'll report you or not report you, whatever you want. But if you're doing this to be nice, or at least what you think is nice . . . " She looked away, blinked quickly. Studied the ground. Let go of his shirt, but he still didn't let go of her hand. "Just be kind. This once. And tell me." This was humiliation. Begging. Asking a stranger to give her a reason to stay. A homicidal stranger at that. "Never mind," she said, and pulled away. "I'm just being stupid."

He grabbed her hand, held it to his heart. "I'm letting you go because I want to do something for you." His voice was rough and low and raw and earnest. The honesty was painful. They both choked on it. Both had difficulty forcing it down.

"What . . . if I want to stay?"

He blinked. "Why would you?"

Because. Because she was a loser. Because it was easier to be with a man who wanted to murder her than be with a man who would only beat her to death.

"My standards are low," she said with an unfunny laugh, and tried to tug her hand away.

He still held firm. "So stay with me." Her eyes flicked to his. "I mean it," he said. "Stay with me. Look inside of my head or whatever you do and see that I mean it."

The inside of his skull, it tasted like roses and barbed wire and butterflies. Switchblades and heroin and grassy green gardens.

He wanted her to stay. Wanted that more than anything in the world, although he wasn't sure why. There was a hole in his heart, which had been there since birth, but somehow he thought she could fill it if she just stayed long enough. Stood by him enough. Maybe fell in love with him, someday, if the stars aligned just right and he was lucky enough to be given a chance in this life. If a monster like him could be loved.

"You're not a monster," she said, and stood on tiptoes to kiss him. He caught his breath, then kissed and bit her lip, twining his arms around her. Pulled her against his body and prayed and prayed and prayed to gods he didn't believe in that this wasn't a dream, that he wasn't somewhere sleeping the glutted slumber of a man who just corpsed a pretty girl. The darkest of afterglows. An afterdark.

"It's real, Lu. I'm real. You're real. And somehow you found me," Montessa whispered, and she felt the heat in Lu's blood then, running like a current under his skin. His want, his desire, his wishes were fanned and ran wild underneath the thin dermis. Her skin responded, her mouth devouring his, and the Wind-That-Was-Not-A-Wind blew around them, tugging at their hair and yanking at their clothes, steam and fire and hurricanes.

"What is all this?" Lu asked between kisses. He didn't want to break his mouth away, didn't want to give up the oxygen Montessa had become, but he needed to know, needed to hear what she thought, what this wildness was. Why he wanted to *hold* a girl instead of *flay* her, and why his arms wrapped so tightly around her waist instead of her throat. "I don't understand," he said, but Montessa was kissing his cheekbones and his eyelids and pulled his head down so she could kiss his forehead, his nose and his chin and his mouth, his mouth, his mouth.

"There's nothing to understand," she whispered, and tugged on his lower lip with her teeth. Her words, they were just right. All he needed. Simplify, Lu. Go on instinct. This was right. It was. It was just, just right.

He wondered if his entire life had been leading up to this. Maybe it had. Maybe this was the beginning of the rest of it.

"The beginning of the end," she answered him, and when Lu smiled, his white teeth made her heart jump and start and stutter in the most beautiful of ways.

"We're going to crash and burn, you know," he told her. He held her close, his face to hers. She smelled like salt and blood and the most beautiful of heats. "They're going to find me, eventually. You'll want to be far away then."

"Oh, baby, we'll go down in flames," she whispered against his mouth. "And I'll be by your side when that happens. Right where I should be."

Lu didn't want to think of the future. Not now. He only wanted to think of the present, and that was almost more than his mind could handle. "I don't believe this is happening," he told her. He murmured it into her hair. He realized her hair was still matted and sticky with dried blood. He pulled back. "You need a bath."

She mock-frowned. "Normally I'm a very clean girl, Lu. For some reason, I was all tied up this week." She laughed, but his brown eyes were serious and concerned and a little bit horrified.

"I mean it, Montessa. Look at you. What I did to you. How can you ever forgive me?"

She twined her arms around his neck, rested her cheek against his. "My Nuclear Lulu. Don't you understand that I know you like nobody else? Of course I forgive you. If you hadn't stolen me . . . " she stopped speaking then. The words were barbed wire, and they hurt. If he hadn't taken her, she'd be waking up with bruised or broken ribs. Perhaps a chipped tooth or two. She'd be taking her clothes off in front of men who were sticky with lust and shame. "I shouldn't thank you," she said, and her voice was so small it sounded like it was going to flicker out. She tried again, stronger. "I shouldn't thank you for what you did. But I feel like I want to. Does that make sense? Because even though I thought you were going to kill me, it was still such a relief. So much better than what my life was."

Her eyes reflected horrors, things he could almost read in her irises, and it made the blood boiling in his veins churn even faster.

"Nobody should be that unhappy," he said.

"You are."

"I was. Not anymore."

He led her to the passenger side, helped her in, and climbed in himself. He drove, and they smiled and were almost shy with each other. It was a first date after the intimacy of intended murder. He stood amid the crows and carcasses, offering her bloodied violets.

Lu saw a place he recognized up ahead. The most spirit-crushing of motels, painted in what had once been beige, with an empty swimming pool in front.

"We'll stop here. It's better than it looks, and I bet nothing sounds better than a hot shower."

"And food," she agreed. "I could eat until I die."

"I'm sorry if I starved you."

"It's okay, Lu."

He paid for a motel room, a cheap place with horrifyingly garish carpet and generic woodland animal pictures on the wall, but the rooms were clean and the tub was spotless. Lu tried to doze on the bed (one of two—he wasn't about to be presumptuous) while Montessa soaped and scrubbed and washed her hair and body with the economy shampoo.

Water never felt so good. Soap never felt so decadent. This shower was a sin, and the water running down her face and body felt better than the hands of any lover.

This was the shower she was never supposed to have—the shower that dead women didn't get to enjoy. It was earned back somehow with her life.

It hit her then, that her life was supposed to *stop*, to *end*, and through a whim of Lu's, this stranger, she was still alive. She could still breathe. Sleep. Make love and enjoy chocolate again and sit through another terrible B monster movie because she loved them so.

It was a second chance. Everything. Montessa could become something, somebody, else. Somebody worthwhile. Maybe she could become the kind of woman she wanted to live for.

Her shower turned salty, and she realized she was crying. It was like the ocean. A baptism of salt. Salt water healed everything, yes?

She wept until she wept everything out. Her bitterness. Her hate. The feelings that she was broken, used up, that there was no reason to exist except to take oxygen away from the wicked. These feelings needed to go. Lu, her lovely, broken, crazy, and wonderful Nuclear Lulu, had chosen her. Was willing to die for her, in order to free her. And that meant something. Meant *she* meant something, and she hadn't meant something before. She was going to live up to it.

She stepped out of the shower feeling fresh and clean and new. A new Montessa. Full of energy and something that felt like hope.

She toweled off, dressed in a pair of Lu's shorts and an old tee. Her clothes were torn and bloodied. They'd dispose of them later.

"I feel different," she said to Lu when she stepped out of the bathroom. "Like things are magical somehow. Like there's so much hope that I could just burst. Just burst from it, Lu!"

He spoke, and it was almost reverent. Yes, *reverent* would be the word she would use. "You're Apocalyptic, Montessa. Apocalyptic Montessa."

She smiled at him, and she could feel the radiance from it.

"And you're my Nuclear Lulu. We're meant to be, my love."

He held out his hand. She walked over and took it. Sparks flew. Magic happened. Nuclear reactors melted down in joy. The world combusted.

CHAPTER ELEVEN

SHE SPENT THE night in Lu's bed, because she didn't want to be alone. It was a new thing to feel lips without fists and her hair pulled without hatred.

"Renan is going to come for me, you know," she told him. She traced his ribs, found a couple that stuck out farther than they should have. Broken how many times? Maybe one day she'd ask. Most likely she wouldn't get the chance.

"Think I'm scared of him?"

Lu had one hand under his head, the other around her. She watched as he studied the ceiling, and it was beautiful. Beautiful plaster, beautiful lighting. Funny how he'd never noticed it before.

"I'm just telling you, Lu. He doesn't like to lose things."

"You're not a thing."

She sighed. Sat up and pulled his T-shirt on. "You're the only one who seems to think that."

"Once you think it, everybody else will follow suit."

She padded to the window and looked out. Highway. A gas station with a fast food joint inside. So unlovely.

She wanted to stay here forever.

"Tell me what the rest of our lives are going to be like," she said and traced her name on the glass with a finger.

"Short. Violent. Full of fear."

"Is that all?"

"Full of love and beauty and adventure."

She bit her lip. Bit it too hard, and tasted blood. "I have to ask you something."

There was a change in her voice as she became *serious*. Montessa heard Lu as he breathed out slowly and tried to relax.

"What?"

She turned toward him, pulling his T-shirt down around her thighs and shuffled her feet nervously. "You didn't kill me."

"Astute girl."

"And you're not going to."

"Not unless you ask me to."

"So do you . . . " She didn't know how to ask it. What to say, really. "Are you still unsatisfied? Since you didn't kill me, do you need to go out and find another girl?"

The words came out in a rush, too close together, cuffed around the wrists and ankles like Lu's Other Girls had been. And she realized she felt a sick stab of jealousy for each one of them, for the pleasure and joy and release they had been able to give him. A sense of peace. A sense of peace that she couldn't.

What kind of woman feels jealous of murdered girls?

Lu must have seen the conflict, because she felt the emotions swing over her features like a bar light. His eyes burned with the heat behind them, and she imagined his fingers longing to trace his knife over her vertebrae, but with tenderness and care, teasing the skin but not tearing it. Not at all.

"Come here," he said, and held out his arms. She walked into them like it was the most normal of things, like they had done it a million times before the world was. Perhaps they had. Perhaps the god that she had always prayed to had really been Lu, and he should have been praying to her. Perhaps they fell, as gods and goddesses so often fell in myth, and only now were they allowed to find each other.

"I want you, okay? Just you. Only you." The words came seemingly easy to his tongue. To his mouth. The truth shouldn't be so accessible, but there it was.

There it was.

"But there are going to be more girls, aren't there? More kills? I mean, you're not going to be able to turn it off like a switch."

She didn't want to make trouble or borrow it, but it was something she needed to know, deep in her little-girl-turned-woman-turned-frightened-little-girl-again heart. Better to face it than wonder. Better to ask than to guess.

"I'll still need to kill, yes."

The air whooshed out of her as though she had been punched. She knew it. Expected it. Expectation didn't make a difference, though. She was still rocked. Still trampled.

"I see," she said. Her voice sounded stable and strong. It didn't betray her at all.

"Don't be like that, baby."

"I know. I'm not trying to. I just feel . . . replaced."

He laughed, flashing his teeth, and Montessa

wondered how many of those lucky murdered girls he'd bitten. "Baby. Montessa. I wish I was better with words, but I'm not. You can't be replaced, do you understand? You're the only thing I want. I don't know how I lived without you."

"But you still need to kill."

"I do. I wish I didn't. I can't seem to help it."

She knew. Nobody wakes up and says, "Why, I think today I will become one of the most hated people in history. A serial killer." She wasn't that naïve. There was a need there. A pull. What were the exact words he used?

"A calling," she said aloud, and Lu nodded.

"A calling, sweetheart. Doing something holy. Taking the evil from the world."

She frowned. "Why me, Lu? Did you think I was evil somehow?"

"No. Not evil. Different. That's all. You were different."

"You watched me and were still going to kill me."

He shrugged. "Them's the breaks, baby. But you know what I think?" He took her by the hand. Kissed her fingers, her ruined wrists.

"What?"

"I think you were a gift from the universe."

"You don't believe in such things."

"I do now." He kissed her, hard, and then stood up. "Let's shower and drop the supply off. Promise me you won't run screaming from the truck as soon as I pull in. That's why I kill the girls first."

"I don't want to get away, Lu."

"All right then."

It was like a first date. They held hands and talked

about silly things. Light things. Things like bubbles and wind chimes, things they almost thought didn't exist in their souls anymore. Lu dropped everything off and filled out his paperwork. Montessa lounged about in the cab and went for a walk around the grounds.

"Where to now?" she asked, and Lu grinned at her.

"Your place."

"My . . . back home?" His face went serious, but his eyes still danced in the way that reminded her of gypsies twisting and burning at the stake. Dangerous. Riveting.

"Yes."

"Why would we go back there? Don't you know Renan . . . "

Lu kissed her fingers. "I think you put too much stock in that man. Give him too much power."

Her face had gone completely translucent. All of the blood had bled out through her tears, flowed from her cuts and bruises and wounds. Years of them.

"Baby," he said, and there was a tone in his voice that told her to look at him. She did, and her eyes were wide with circles of deadness inside.

"Baby," he said again, softer. "Do you think I'll let him hurt you?"

"I don't think you'd mean to."

"Montessa. I won't. I promise. But more than that, you won't."

"Lu."

"His time is over, Montessa. You need to let him go. Erase that evil from the world."

Her eyes locked with his, and Lu nodded before turning his attention back to the road.

"You'll see," he said. He turned slowly on the

winding road, following a path he knew was unfamiliar to Montessa. "It'll be like magic. It'll be holy. It'll be one of the best experiences of your life."

She didn't know what to say, but her heart swelled and burst. It kept trying to race, but she blinked and breathed and pulled her knees up to her chest. Wrapped her fingers around her seatbelt.

She didn't speak for two more states.

"Will you help me?" she asked. They were only a few hours from her home.

"Of course I will. I'll always help you. Keep you safe. As safe as I can, anyway. I'll be by your side forever."

"Forever," she repeated and swallowed.

"Until the end of time. For as long as we have."

CHAPTER TWELVE

LU HANDED HER the knife, and she took it with a respect that made her even more stunning in his eyes. She held it gently, ran her finger carefully across the blade, and held it to her face to inspect it. Her breath fogged up the metal and Lu grit his teeth to keep from moaning.

"From your father to you, and now you'll let me use it?"

"For your first kill. For any kill you want. Until you find something that you like better. Or always."

They parked far away, walking to her house. It was dark. The gravel crunched beneath their feet. Montessa held Lu's hand and ran her finger across the bones of his knuckles.

"This is . . . crazy," she said, keeping her voice low.

"This is what is meant to be," he answered back.

How many times had he prowled this area? He knew it backward and forward. But Montessa still knew it better. They strolled under streetlights, through darkness, past addicts and drunks and frightened runaways, through alleys and parks and cemeteries.

"This is a long way to walk alone. Dangerous, too. I can't believe he made you do it so often."

"Oh, don't be so harsh," she said, her voice light. "Really, what could happen?"

She laughed, but Lu didn't. He remembered beating her in the head with the wrench and felt a punch in his gut, his muscles pulling together too tightly. He grabbed her, pulled her to him, and kissed her hard.

"I'm sorry," he said. He held her close, nipped her ear. "I'm sorry, I'm sorry, I'm sorry."

She held him back. "I know, darling. I know." She smiled at him, and it was real. Teeth and joy, and the sorrow was erased from her face, everywhere but her eyes. "Let's go do this, okay? Be with me, Lu. I need you for this."

He nodded, and they were on their way again, fingers laced.

Her home looked lonely. The grass was too long, and her flowers were already starting to wilt. She shook her head.

"This place is all the joy I had," she said, and they skirted around to the back. Lu watched as she peeked in her window, returned, and said she saw Renan and a froth of black hair on the pillow next to him.

"He has company," she said and frowned.

"I'm sorry, baby."

"It's okay. It's not like he wasn't doing it before. But . . . I don't know." She looked at Lu, and her eyes were too bright. "I was *kidnapped*, Lu. Tied to a metal chair. And he—"

He pulled her close and kissed her forehead. "We'll make them pay," he whispered.

She took the spare key from a fake rock in the garden.

"Those are terrible places to hide keys," Lu said. He bounced on his toes in anxious delight. "Everybody knows about them."

"I know," she said. "Half the time, I'm hoping somebody will break in and kill me anyway."

The key slid in smoothly, without a sound. She unlocked the door quietly, slipped inside, with Lu following her on sneakered feet.

Lu chloroformed two rags.

"I usually don't use it," he had told her earlier. "It's your first time, and it's pretty tricky until you get the hang of it. No mistakes or regrets. Okay?"

"Okay."

Now she held her cloth tightly in her white fingers, looking at Lu nervously. He winked and grinned. She smiled back. He pointed at her and then at Renan. Himself and the girl.

He's yours, Lu mouthed, and she nodded as she studied Renan's sleeping form, his shaved head and ratty mustache. The softness of his lips belied the hardness of the rest of him.

She couldn't look at the woman who belonged to the tight, black curls on the pillow. She wouldn't. There would be no ill will if she wasn't here right now. Wrong place, wrong time. She closed her mind, closed her heart to the sleeping woman. She didn't exist anymore.

Renan's brows bunched up, his lips pursed, and he turned in his sleep like he heard them. Perhaps he had.

It was time.

She looked at Lu, and he looked back.

Now? His raised eyebrows seemed to ask.

She nodded. *Now.*

She held the chloroformed rag over Renan's nose and mouth.

His eyes opened, too wide, staring at something in his nightmares, something standing at the foot of his bed or his mother's undressed, old lovers, or whatever it was that made his eyes bug out and strange sounds come from his throat. He grabbed at Montessa, but she stepped deftly aside.

"Renan, sweetheart. It's me. I'm home. Shhhh." He relaxed slightly at her voice, but then scrabbled at her hands, at the cloth, at his face. His muscles were already confused and weak with sleep, and the chloroform effective. "Shhh, darling. Just some medicine for you. I missed you, sweetheart. I'm so glad to be home."

The lies tasted like her lies always tasted. At first, they had been bitter and acrid, but she was so used to them by now that they tasted sweet like frosting. *I'll never leave you, Renan. I love you. I've never been happier.*

He struggled and she soothed, and soon his dark eyes fluttered shut again. His face was slack in a way she had never seen before. This was more than sleep. This was something darker and longer lasting.

She realized she'd started panting, and pushed her sweaty hair out of her face. She looked at Lu. He was crouched over the body of the woman, watching Montessa carefully.

"You did fine," he said, and Montessa jumped at the sound of his voice.

"Shhh! Quiet!"

He grinned at her. "Why? They're out, baby."

He lifted the woman's arm by her wrist and

dropped it. It fell heavily on the bed with the sound of wet meat.

Montessa bit her lip, staring at Renan and his new woman de jour. "And now we . . . what?"

"Kill them."

"Lu, I don't think—"

"You can do it. You know you need to. He saw you. He'll come after you."

She chilled, felt her stomach twist, and suddenly felt like she needed to use the restroom.

"Montessa. You can do this."

He turned back to the woman, took a second knife out of its sheath, and traced it along her dark skin.

Montessa took a deep breath. Another. Took Lu's beautiful knife from his first and most important kill. Held it to her heart as if it were a stuffed animal from a boyfriend. As if it were the most exquisite thing she had ever owned.

"Where do I start?"

"Make it quick. It'll be easier for both of you. You can slit his throat if you'd like."

She felt herself go pale. Put her hand over her mouth.

Lu nodded. "I didn't think so. That's something to ease into. Garrote him, baby. Or go up under his ribs and into his heart. I'll show you where."

"I'll be right back," she said, and put the knife on the bed. She walked out of the room and down the hall to the kitchen. Funny how this was her house, but it seemed so unfamiliar. She knew where things were and what room led into what room and where all of the doorways would take her, but it wasn't her home. It was a place she had never been before. An alien land. A dream.

Her feet took her to the fridge. She opened it and reached for the Diet Coke shoved in the back. There was one left and little else. Of course Renan wouldn't go shopping. He'd wait for her to come back so she could do it. He'd tell one of his little whores to do it instead.

She popped the top and drank a long swallow. Two. Held the cold can to her cheek and tried to pull herself together.

This was death. Not playtime. Not the sad little revenge of a teenager. This was murder.

She wasn't a murderer. She was a lot of things. Sad. Tired, mostly. Special. That last one made her laugh. Sure, she had a few little parlor tricks, but everybody had their secrets. The things that made them tick.

Renan never made her feel like she was special.

She was singled out for his abuse, but that wasn't being special. And he hit the other women, too. She'd seen enough split lips and sunglasses at night to know he was lavishing his particular type of charm on more than just herself.

She wasn't even special enough to be his only punching bag.

His only lover.

She was his maid. His housekeeper. Somebody who kept the lights turned on.

Renan was her daddy, only much better looking.

She shut the fridge and drained the rest of her drink. Threw the can in the recycling bin, and then smiled bitterly because nobody would ever recycle here again. Or clean, or do housework, or pay bills.

She was ready to kill him.

The woman was already sliced open by the time

she came back. Montessa stared, the scarlet insides looking wet and ravenous and almost sexual. Lu's hands were red nearly up to the elbows and his eyes were slightly unfocused, the pupils large.

"He'll come to soon," he said. He wiped his forehead with the back of his hand, smearing blood across his face in unintentional war paint. "You'd better hurry."

"I'm ready."

"Need some help?"

She shook her head, and he nodded. Communication without words. Forget being baptized earlier in salt: This was Montessa's baptism in blood.

She kissed the tip of Lu's First Kill knife, let her lips linger. Moved them carefully, saying a prayer. She used to pray as a little girl. She'd almost forgotten that, but it seemed right.

She set the tip of the knife on Renan's sternum, wondering if his skin was warm, wondering how long it would take to cool.

"Not there. More to the side. Under. Beneath the ribs, to the heart." Lu's voice. His calm, melodious voice. Calm and beautiful, her True North. She repositioned her knife. "Atta girl. And lean hard. All of your weight. It'll be more difficult than you think."

The knife was so sharp. So cold and clean. Seeing the way that Renan's blood oozed under its steely touch, it was like being plunged into too-cold water. Falling unexpectedly into the river and scrabbling over the rocks, coughing out water and oxygen and what was left of youthful hope and optimism. Barking up pieces of lung and tissue. Good-feeling and organs.

She watched the pulse in Renan's neck, thought about the way she used to rest with her head on his chest, listening to his heart. It was the only time that she remembered really being happy with him. Knowing that he was there, alive, that his arm was thrown around her . . .

A woman as lonely as Montessa should really just get a dog.

The scream surprised her, a small feral sound somewhere deep in her throat, bursting up from the broken places inside and screaming out through her mouth. She leaned on the knife, threw her weight against it, pushing into the floor with the balls of her feet, and felt the knife push, push, push until there was blood and her hands were slick. It was on her face, running down her neck. Renan made a sound, the most terrible of sounds, the most heart-wrenching and sickening of sounds, jerking and choking, and then there was nothing.

Nothing.

"Okay, baby?"

She couldn't answer. Her hands were glued to the bloody knife, wrapped around the handle so tight she could feel her blood pulsing through her fingers. Carrying oxygen. Carrying nutrients. Not useless like Renan's blood now was.

Lu put one red hand on hers, and she realized she was sobbing.

"Come here," he said, and gently tugged her hands from the blade. He wrapped her arms around his waist, wrapped his arms around her. He bent his forehead down to touch hers. "I'm here," he said and let her shake.

She tried to cover her face with her hands, but Lu held them down firmly.

"They're bloody," he said, and she collapsed against him again, crying, holding onto his body through the thin cotton of his shirt.

Her tears soaked his clothes, and Lu became afraid. Afraid that this was too much for her, that it wasn't the liberation that he had experienced, but something frightening and ugly and evil.

Maybe it wasn't cleansing, he thought, and held her even tighter. *Maybe I broke her. What if she thinks she's damned?*

The shaking intensified, so hard that he felt he was going to lose her, that she was going to shake apart into pieces of bones and sinews.

"Baby? I'm sorry. I thought this would help. I thought—"

Was this what despair felt like? Absolute horror? Because if this was more than she could handle, if this had turned her into a monster, or worse, made her realize he was one himself, then she would go.

She would go. And he would have nothing left.

The shaking and the sounds. The tears and the torrential wailing from Montessa. The room itself began to quiver, the bed and the dresser shook, and the now-familiar Wind-That-Was-Not-A-Wind blew through the room, blowing bits of meat and shreds of skin from the bed. Blew a hat down that he realized was Montessa's. Shattered the mirror on the wall.

"Montessa. My love. You need to pull yourself together."

This was it. She was breaking. Her first kill had thrown her right over the edge into insanity, and he was the one who caused it.

She pulled back and looked at him. The teeth that split her face wide. The way her eyes . . . danced.

She was laughing. *Laughing.*

"He's gone, Lu. I did it. I killed him."

She put her hands to her face, and this time, Lu didn't stop her. She laughed and sobbed, and Renan's blood ran down her face with her tears. A bloody teardrop slid into her mouth, and Lu bent close and kissed it away.

"Are you all right?"

She gulped in deep breaths, looked at Renan and the corpse that lay beside him. No, looked at the two corpses lying together. She tasted blood. Knew it wasn't hers. Thought that the last time she had seen Renan, she had tasted blood, too. "Yours tastes better," she murmured, and her legs gave out.

Lu caught her and helped her to the ground.

"Don't fade out on me. Look at me."

"I killed him," she said again. Her voice was getting faint. She looked down at her clothes, knew they were ruined. Knew there were stains that would never come out, never. Out of your heart, out of your shirt.

"Come on," Lu said, and helped her up. He mostly carried her to the shower, and turned the water on.

"How do you like it?"

"Hot. It's never hot enough."

He grinned, the blood splatter looking like shiny freckles in the light. "I can make it as hot as you want. Hotter."

He pulled off his shirt, stepped out of his jeans. The water warmed, steamed, and he peeled Montessa out of her clothes. She stood there like a broken doll or an obedient little girl.

"In," Lu said. She stepped into the tub. Lu followed and pulled the shower curtain shut.

"Warm enough?" he asked her.

She was still shivering. She thought she'd never be warm again. All of her hot blood had seeped out with Renan's. All of her warmth. "No," she said. Her lips felt sticky. She turned her face to the showerhead and watched the water run red at her feet.

Lu narrowed his eyes, and the water heated up even more. Their skin turned red, mottled, but Montessa only sighed.

"Thank you. I think I love you, Lu."

He washed her, firmly and with love, getting all of the blood and bad memories off. He washed her hair with her own shampoo. Turned her to face him and kissed her lips gently. Lu washed himself with a dead man's soap. Turned off the water and dried them with a dead man's towel.

"They're my towels, too, you know," she said, but her voice was still shaking.

"I know they are."

"This . . . this is my house."

"I know, baby."

"I just exorcised it."

"You did."

They dressed. She in her clothes, he in Renan's. Everything was too big, but clean. Lu wondered if Montessa had washed them last, or if Renan had.

"Of course I did. Or maybe one of his girls. That man wouldn't know how to start a washing machine."

They sat at the table. Ate some cold cuts and Lu had a beer. Montessa wished there was more Diet Coke.

"Better pack a bag," Lu said. He looked around the house, the kitchen. He'd seen inside so many times, but it was different when he was actually here, sitting in the chair.

"Kinda like playing house, isn't it?" Montessa's eyes had refocused. The glow was starting to come back. Her hands had stopped trembling. She pushed her wet hair out of her face.

"Kinda is."

"Maybe that can be our dream, Lu. Our own house. I want a purple one."

"Backed up to the river."

"That would be nice."

"A garden?"

"Of course."

"How about otters?"

"Now you're just being silly, Lu."

"But I really want otters."

It would never happen, this dream. They'd never settle. Never be safe. They'd have to move and move and move, because staying meant getting caught, and getting caught meant getting separated.

Lu realized he had never known real terror until now. He thought he knew it, thought he understood and breathed it in, but that hadn't been the case. Discomfort instead of horror. Annoyance instead of misery. The idea of being separated from Montessa—from his other half—made his eyes bleed. He bled water from his eyes.

"Don't cry, Lulu. I love you."

"I love you, too."

She kissed him, a long, gentle kiss. The kind of kiss meant to take place in meadows with picnics and sunshine. The kind of kiss that, in any other situation and with any other couple, would mean forever. But here and now, with her boyfriend dead in the other room, it was filled with a strange sorrow.

"I'll miss you," she whispered against his mouth. "I've never missed anyone before."

"You haven't lost me yet," he said.

"Yes, but I will."

She stuffed her clothes into a bag. She tossed a black duffle to Lu, and he stuffed Renan's clothes into it with deft, mechanical speed. He was a man used to getaways. Used to taking what he wanted and then walking away while everything burned behind him.

"Will it bother you to see me in his clothes?" he asked her. He kept his eyes on his task, seemingly unconcerned, but she could feel how he roiled and steamed and burned inside. Would this drive her away? Was this a terrible mistake? Should he have taken Renan out instead of her? Was she damaged? Would she blame him for this life? She had been a victim before. Now she was an accomplice.

"Don't go nuclear on me, Lulu."

"I don't know if I'll ever get used to you knowing what I'm thinking."

"You will, darling."

She stood in her house one last time, and thought of her things, none of which meant anything. Montessa thought of the bodies in the bedroom, which meant even less. She took a deep breath and took Lu's hand.

They left the house without a word. She didn't look back, but held tightly to her bag and to Lu. She heard the rumble of flames as they erupted behind her. Knew the fire was gnawing at the skeleton of its structure.

She bit her lip, concentrating, and called up a fierce wind that fed the fire. She felt the heat at her back, saw her shadow dance before her. Wild and free and fierce. Her shadow had a knife in its hand that glowed like the divine guiding star.

She had never known shadows could smile before.

Lu's shadow grinned and writhed, as well, every bit the demon his father always said he was. A demon of beauty. A demon of deliverance. She watched their unholy celebration, shadow hands and fate intertwined.

CHAPTER THIRTEEN

LU DROVE, AND Montessa sat quietly, playing with his First Kill knife, which had now become her First Kill knife, as well.

Finally, he broke the silence. "Doing okay?"

"Yes. Thank you."

"No problem."

He remembered stabbing his father, over and over and over, that primal sound he had made, the sweet, unfamiliar-now-familiar feel of flesh and bone and muscle give, give, giving under the blade.

"It was that good," Montessa said. It wasn't a question.

"It was. Yours?"

"I'm still processing."

"Of course."

He drove through most of the night without a word. His knee jiggled. He tapped his fingers on the steering wheel. Lu was afraid he'd lost her.

They pulled over, and both crawled into the tiny, built-in bed together. He wrapped his arms around her, and she threw her leg over his, her arm over his chest.

"Just a little warmer, please?"

The room heated up immediately. She heard the currents of electricity and fire zipping through his veins. Any more heat and her clothes would begin to steam, her skin would sizzle and char, her hair singe. It felt good. It felt so very, very good.

"Goodnight, Nuclear Lulu."

"Sleep sweet, Apocalyptic Montessa."

She fell into sleep like she was diving off a cliff and slamming face first into pavement. Dreams of blood coated her tongue. Montessa wore a fine red dress that used to be white once, she thought, and long gloves of crimson coated her arms past her elbow. Renan and her father and her cousins and everybody else turned into paper dolls that burst into the most beautiful of flames.

Lu didn't sleep. He buried his face in Montessa's hair and listened to every gasp, to every murmur and cry she made. He licked her tears away and wondered why he had met her now, when everything was reaching its conclusion. He didn't have much longer, he knew. And now he had brought her with him.

She could still claim to be a victim. That's what she should do. Come screaming out of the wilderness one day, wild-eyed and ragged, telling how the man had taken her and murdered her love. Then how he'd burned her place to the ground while she was tied up and how she was forced to watch. It would be hard to start over, but she would be able to do it. Montessa was beautiful and soft and fragile, but she had a core made of steel. Made of sterner stuff than most people would believe.

Besides, her mama always said she was special.

"Lu, I'm starving. Let's find somewhere for breakfast. Come on!"

She was aglow. Alight. A nuclear holocaust of delicious energy. She flitted around the cab like a butterfly on speed, a firefly on crack. The air fairly buzzed with her delight.

"You woke up perky."

"And you didn't wake up at all. But we'll talk about that later. Now feed me!" She knelt down beside the bed, kissed his mouth, his cheeks and chin and mouth again. "I have plans, Lu."

"Tell me."

"Food first."

They found a tiny diner in a worn-out town, where Lu drowned himself in coffee while Montessa ordered a Diet Coke. When breakfast came, she ate like she'd been starved for years.

"Montessa, I know how to get you out of this."

"I don't want to get out of it."

"I know what to do. You're strong enough to—"

"I said no, Lu."

"I can't lose you. Now that I have you, I can't let you go."

She smiled at him. "So don't. And listen. You're a terrible listener." She slapped a piece of paper on the table, and then a map. "Tell me where your next deliveries are? What routes you'll take?"

He pointed. "Here. Here to here. And then most likely this way, though I'm not sure yet. Why?"

Her smile, it was beautiful. It was sweet and very

nearly sanctified and burned with demon fire at the same time.

"I have a kill here. A few in this area. Some people that I want to see . . . gone."

Their eyes met over the breakfast table. Intense. Burning. A force of nature meets a force of nature and turns into an irrevocable storm. The lights flickered in the diner.

"I can save you from this," Lu said one more time. "I'll go down. It's my time. You can distance yourself from me."

"And live what kind of life? I see it. I See it. I know how it's going to end. And we'll be together. Isn't that what you want? It's what I want."

She smiled again, and it was disarming. He wondered how she had been as a little girl, asking for sweets or playing with her doll or . . .

Most likely none of those things had happened. Her childhood was too similar to his. No sweets. No dolls. Just games that needed to be played with people stronger than they were. Doors that shut with that horrifying click when nobody else was around. Feelings of confusion and shame and that pain, pain, pain that never fully went away, made it difficult to sit and walk.

There was a sound, a hissing sound, and Lu realized his hand was burning into the wooden table. He pulled it back quickly.

"Yes," she said, and her too-pale eyes went dark. "Them. That's who I'm going after. All of them. Will you help me?"

"I will."

She laughed, and it was bubbles, pixie dust, and the

genuine delight of a girl who had been given the most precious of gifts. She ran around the table and threw her arms around Lu.

"Thank you. Thank you," she said, and Lu held her, ran his hands over her hair and the scabs on her wrists. He kissed her collarbone and scooted over so she could sit beside him.

"I could hold you forever," he said, and blushed. Words never said before. Feelings never felt before. His emotions had been char and ash, but suddenly there was something shiny in the world. Innocent.

"I'm not innocent."

"You're innocent."

And today would be one of the best days of their lives. He'd think back to this moment in the diner, when she laughed and spread an unsightly amount of orange marmalade on her toast, and they laughed and planned and plotted. What to wear. How to find their new victims. How to hunt down and stalk each and every last one.

"I was careful at first," Lu admitted. "Took a lot of time and care. Pick up the victim here, kill her in the truck, drop the pieces off somewhere else. Mostly people nobody would miss. Kept things clean. But lately, it hasn't been that way."

"How's it been?"

"See a girl and grab her. Kill her and dump her. You were different, though. I watched you. Knew you. Came in and watched you dance, saw the way you treated your coworkers."

"Did you like watching me dance?"

He frowned. "I didn't like watching other guys watching you dance."

"They're harmless. Just men and women out for a good time, someplace they can forget. And be forgotten."

"Doesn't matter. I still didn't like it." He leaned back in the booth. Stretched. "That's funny, too, because I usually don't care. You're a mark. You have nothing to do with me."

"Maybe you knew, even then. That we were meant to be together."

"Maybe."

They paid their tab and gathered up her list.

"My Kill List," she said, and they both grinned, both felt like children standing in front of the witch's gingerbread and peppermint stick house.

"Your Kill List," he agreed.

They made love in the cab. Refueled and set off into the bright, bright morning.

CHAPTER FOURTEEN

THEY DROPPED THEIR next load off, and spent a day playing in the sunshine, hiking through the forest. Montessa pointed at the birds and squirrels and marveled at the beauty of it all.

Tiny hearts. Tiny blood vessels. Tiny, tiny veins.

"Does it ever get old?" she asked. "Do you ever get tired of killing?"

"No," he said, and the sound of his voice, the weight of his words, told her he was speaking truth. Their next kill would be tonight. One of her cousins, a devil named Emmanuel, with a squeaky voice and hands too large for his body.

"I'm going to cut his hands off and stuff them in his mouth," she said. "Make him bite down on every finger until it breaks."

"You can do that, but he'll bleed out pretty soon."

Montessa looked at him, and he shrugged.

"Just saying, Montessa. You can do all of these things. Kill and then dismember. Dismember then kill. Whatever you choose."

She was thoughtful about this. "Just kill," she said about two hours later. "I don't want to lose myself in all of this. Do you ever lose yourself, Lu?"

"No. I just find myself." He smiled with those wicked white teeth, and her heart bounced in her chest. Shuddered like a heart that had not yet felt steel under the ribcage.

"How would you have killed me?" she asked.

"You really want to talk about it?"

"I want to know."

"Softly, I think. Like I said, you weren't like the others."

"With your knife?"

"Probably."

"Tell me."

Lu wondered. Wondered why she wanted to know, why it was important. Maybe she wanted to know if he thought about it still. If he regretted not taking the chance when he had it. Maybe this was love to her—pain and abuse. Maybe she wasn't used to the softness. He wasn't used to it either.

"I would have kept your mouth duct taped so you wouldn't scream."

"Okay."

"And . . . I don't know. Maybe I'd pull the truck over and take you outside. Probably. It depends on how much you would have fought."

"Where?"

"Somewhere with trees. Remember where we stopped back with the pines? Where you got tired and fell down? Somewhere like that."

"Or there?"

"Or there."

His voice, it was soft. Melodious. A voice that was created to sing songs with a guitar, to hush babies to sleep in the middle of the night. The universe knew these things, even if Lu didn't.

"I'd take you outside, and I'd hold you so close to me."

"Yes?"

"I'd take my knife . . . "

"The First Kill knife?"

"Yes. The First Kill knife. I'd slip it under your ribs into your heart, like you did to Renan."

Her lips made an O.

"Or perhaps into your lungs from behind. Hold you in my arms and—"

"Stab me in the back?"

"It doesn't sound nearly as romantic that way."

"It isn't."

"But the way you'd fall," he explained, and hoped she understood. Prayed she would. Send the vision rolling from his brain to hers in waves, pushed it into her skull with all of the force of his mental hands. "You'd go limp in my arms, looking into my eyes, and it would be the most . . . intimate thing that ever happened to you. The last thing you'd see is me. The last gaze you hold would be mine. And my attention would be totally, 100% focused on you, my love."

She frowned. "I almost feel like I'm disappointing you by living."

"Never. I want you to live forever. With me, always."

Night fell, and they crept toward the apartment. It was in a bad part of a bad city. Montessa picked her way through trash and wrinkled her nose at the smell of urine in the gutter.

"Maybe we should just let him live," she said. "It would be punishment enough."

He lived upstairs, and the stone steps were steep enough that her heart shivered a little.

"I don't like heights," she whispered to Lu. "If we get caught tonight, you should know this."

"I'm afraid of clowns."

"Now that's just weird. Hush up, baby. Give me a few minutes."

She climbed the steps. Bit her lip and blew out her breath. Pulled her neckline down a few inches and knocked on the door. Her hand, it felt diseased from touching the rotted wood. She could feel the germs and filth swarming its way up her arm, across her shoulder. The way he had always made her feel. She glanced down the steps toward Lu's hiding place, and then squared her shoulders. She heard it was supposed to make her braver. It didn't.

She knocked again.

"What?"

She heard the voice through the door. It sounded older. Meaner. But she could still hear the same tones in it, still recognized it from so long ago. Heavens knew it showed up in enough nightmares for it to be heartbreakingly familiar.

"Emmanuel? Honey, is that you?" She made her voice sweet. Sweet enough to drip sugar water, to entice his hands and tongue and everything else that made him human.

"Who are you?"

"It's Montessa. We used to be . . . close."

The door opened, but the cheap, metal chain stretched across the opening. "Yeah?"

His eye peered out through the crack of the door, and Montessa nearly puked. How many times had she seen that before? She swallowed hard, smoothed her clothes nervously. When she smiled, it was brilliant. "Remember me? It was a long time ago."

Lust. She could feel it rolling off him in waves. She wavered and steadied herself on the railing. He remembered her.

"Are you alone, baby?" she asked. She was on autopilot. Time to play Ruby from the strip club, to wear that mask. Montessa was nowhere to be seen anymore. She was tucked in bed, wearing sweet striped pajamas and sleeping the peaceful sleep of the weary. Ruby was in charge now, and Ruby would protect her.

"I'm alone."

"Can I come in? I was in town and hoped maybe you and I could have a little fun."

She slid her hand to her back pocket, gripped the handle of the Killing Knife. It was fairly singing. She felt the energy sliding up her arm like the most sensuous of caresses. Felt her eyes go large and huge with her own type of lust. Lusting for body and lusting for blood, it was the same.

The door shut. She heard the chain. It opened again all of the way, and she saw Emmanuel standing there in an old T-shirt and dirty cargo pants. "Come in," he said.

She peeked into his brain, saw the confusion and delight there. Felt the darkness welling up from somewhere deep within. Montessa saw herself as a child, tiny and scared, curled up in her bed, holding a long-forgotten stuffed animal tightly in her arms. Felt the wicked joy washing over him, like soup in a bowl, sloshing over the sides and making her hands sticky. "That's right. Remember all of the fun we had, Manny."

She shut the door behind her, taking care to leave it unlocked. Her hands shook, but she kept her Ruby face on. Interested. Hardly repulsed at all.

"Want to go in the other room? I don't have as much time as I'd like. Perhaps we could get started."

He couldn't believe his luck. Couldn't believe that tonight, just some random night, one of his favorite memories would show up on his doorstep, begging for more. He knew that, even though she had struggled and fought, pretending to hate it, she had wanted more. "The room's back here."

He turned and walked down the hall, tripping over dirty clothes and half-eaten food. He didn't take her hand. Didn't feign concern. Nice to know some things didn't change.

I'm in charge, Montessa reminded herself. Her skin felt clammy, and the room spun, but she touched the handle of the knife in her back pocket again. Her center. Told herself she could do this, that she chose this, that she was bigger now than she had been then. She was nearly eye-level with Emmanuel, but somehow this didn't make it much better.

Now she was closer to his mouth. Closer to his teeth and tongue.

I'm going to kill you, she thought, and was able to take a step forward. Followed him to the bedroom. Her heart beat and beat and beat so hard that she could see her shirt move with the force of it, but she was strong. She had faced down Renan. She could do this, too.

His room was filthy. It reeked of sweat and body odor and being closed-in for too long.

He sat on the dirty sheets. "Well? What exactly do you want to do?"

She showed her teeth, was pretty sure that it presented as a smile. "Take off your shirt, darling. And then get on the bed. Turn around."

His hands. Too thick. Too clumsy. Heavy and awkward as slabs of meat. She turned away while he pulled his shirt over his head. Put a hand to her stomach.

"Sick?"

"No, Manny. Just butterflies."

He grinned, goofy, still disbelieving of his good luck, turned around, and showed his white, acne-covered back.

She raised the knife as she touched his skin with her hand. The knife hovered over the muscle in his back. She moved it to his spine, to his neck.

She shook.

She couldn't do this.

"Montessa?"

"Yes, darling?"

"Are you going to do something soon?"

"Of course."

"Good, because I don't like to wait." He laughed. "Remember how I don't like to wait?"

"I remember."

He didn't hear the change in her voice. The hardness. If he had, perhaps he would have changed his tactic. He would have said, "Oh, Montessa, I'm so sorry. Please forgive me for what I did. I'm so ashamed. It never should have happened."

But instead he said, "You were always one of my favorites, you know."

She froze. "What?"

"You were always one of my favorites. Maybe my very favorite. There were a couple of others who were almost as nice, but you?"

"There were more? More little girls?"

"Girls. Boys. I'm not gay or nothing, but you take what you can get. A kid is a kid, right? But you? Oh, you were something special."

"So I've been told."

"Your daddy said that, too. Told us. All of us. He was the one who—"

Montessa grabbed his head, jerked it back. Leaned over him and drew the knife along his throat.

Poorly.

Emmanuel screamed and bucked her off, scrabbling at his neck. He whirled toward Montessa, blood squirting through his fingers and landing on her face, her neck, in her eyes.

She stabbed at him again, in the neck, missing the artery, and her hand slid through the blood. She lost her grip on the knife, and it fell to the ground. She was crying, sobbing loudly, and dove after it. She grabbed it by the blade, and it bit deeply into her hand.

Emmanuel choked and gurgled, clawing at his neck with one hand and reaching for Montessa with the other.

She staggered to her feet, then slipped in his blood and went down hard.

A flurry behind her, and Lu's sneakers hit the floor, skidding through the blood and stopping abruptly. She pushed her hair out of her eyes and watched him grab

Emmanuel from behind and expertly cut his throat. Lu threw the body on the bed, where it jerked and spasmed.

He grabbed Montessa by the upper arm and dragged her to her feet. "Are you okay?" he asked, running his hands over her arms and legs. He checked her face, her neck, and then pulled her to his chest. "Montessa. Are you all right?"

"I'm okay. My hand."

He grabbed it, saw the depth of the cut. He ripped a strip off of the bed sheet and wrapped it around her hand. It crimsoned instantly.

"Is he dead?" she asked.

"He's dead. We have to go. Now."

He grabbed her wrist, pulling her through the pooling blood and through the hallway. She looked back and saw their bloody footprints, saw herself running down the hallway forever and into eternity, leaving nothing but blood, blood, blood behind her.

"We need to clean up," she said, but Lu was pushing her out the shabby front door and down the cement stairs.

"No time. Bad kill. We need to leave."

They pelted down the street, and Montessa gasped at the *whoosh* of the building going up in flames.

"Lu! There were other people in that building!"

"This will give us time."

"Not at the expense of innocent people!"

He pulled her into the hedges, dragged her down the back pathways.

"You screwed up, Montessa. You're new, it's okay. I should have gotten there earlier. But we don't have time to clean up. I could hear the fighting and yelling from outside. The neighbors were looking out their windows."

"But—"

"Look at you. You've covered in blood. I just saved your life."

Sirens. They flattened low to the ground behind the hedgerows, watched the fire truck and the police race toward the fire.

"Take off your shirt."

"What?"

"Take it off. Now."

They peeled off their tops. Lu gave his to Montessa.

"Not as bloody. Now we walk. Holding hands, like lovers."

He carried her bunched up shirt in his hand, and they strolled carelessly down the road, just another couple out under the stars.

"Do you believe in soul mates?" he asked her.

"Is this the time for that?"

"Your body language is stressed. You look ready to bolt. It makes you suspicious."

"So we'll talk about soul mates."

"Sure."

"Want to ask me about Santa Claus, too?"

"I take it you're not a believer."

She scuffed her bloodied Keds across the sidewalk. "It's a romantic thought, but it's a load of bunk."

"Why is that?"

She shrugged, looking at the sky and the smoke starting to cover the stars. Black smoke. Beautiful smoke. Lu smoke.

She smiled, and it took his breath away, made his stomach ache more than any hunger pains or punches in the gut ever could. He held her hand tighter, laced his fingers even more closely. The blood was sticky and itchy, but her fingers were long and slim and absolutely wonderful.

"What kind of person would want me for a soul mate, Lu? To be stuck with me forever, regardless? That just sounds like a bad deal all around."

"Don't say that."

"And what if my soul mate is somebody awful? Somebody cruel? What if it's Renan or somebody like him? And I can't get away, no matter what. Cosmically trapped."

"Do you think it would really be like that?"

"I wouldn't expect anything, I don't think."

They were almost to the truck. Lu swung her hand playfully. "The thing about soul mates is that they're a good fit, baby."

She looked at him, her eyes reflecting the starlight. "I take it you're a believer, Lu."

He smiled, and kissed her bloodied hand. "There's a Chinese legend about the Red Thread of Fate. Have you heard it?"

"No."

"Two people who are destined to be together are tied together by the red thread. And the thread tangles, and it pulls and stretches, but the idea is that it never breaks."

"Never? No matter what?"

"No matter what."

They reached the truck. He opened her door and helped her inside. Jogged around and climbed into his seat. Lu started the engine, pulled onto the road. Reached for her hand again, and she gladly gave it to him. "You're meant for me, Montessa. I never would have thought it. And I'm meant for you. Our paths in life, they were following this red thread. We're meant to be."

"You really believe that?"

"I do. I've never believed something so firmly in my life."

Montessa put her feet on the dash, holding Lu's hand. She needed to wash up, but not quite yet. She'd never heard such beautiful words, words spoken with such intent and earnestness. She poked around inside of his head and knew he had been following his red thread all of his life. That he had held to it when the demons were being beat out of him, when he was the kid with the funny eyes in his California school, when he lay in his room at night knowing he would never be loved for the monster he was. Except that just maybe . . .

The thread led right to Montessa, tied firmly around her bloodied wrist. And neither of them would ever let it go.

CHAPTER FIFTEEN

HER NIGHTMARES STARTED that night.

She washed off as best as she could, but could feel Emmanuel's blood seeping into the cracks of her hands. It was as if her skin was no longer waterproof, and the blood soaked through into her body.

His ham hands hit her hard in the eye socket, and she screamed.

"Shh, baby. I'm here." Lu had his arms wrapped around her, but it still wasn't close enough.

"I'm cold," she said, and he warmed the air around them. Warmed the little built-in bed. Warmed her heart when he pressed his lips against her neck.

"Go back to sleep."

She dreamed of Emmanuel's freakishly large hands clutching at his throat while his blood spurted. The cut wasn't clean. The cut wasn't sure. She felt the larynx grind under the blade of the First Kill knife. Sickly. Gristle. The high-pitched shrieking, squealing, screaming that was Emmanuel. He had been human before that, but after her botched murder, he had become a stuck farm animal. A screeching pig. So much meat.

"You're crying out in your sleep, baby."

"I'm sorry."

"Don't be. I know how it is at first."

"Does it ever get better?"

He kissed her sweaty hair. "Eventually."

She turned in his arms, buried her nose in that perfect spot in his neck. "I love you, Lu."

"I love you, too."

"They're going to find us, aren't they?"

"Yes."

She thought for a while, running her fingers through Lu's soft, dark hair. "Even faster now that I messed that one up, huh."

He traced his name on her shoulder with his finger. She was so fine. China fine. Delicate bone. They'd shatter so easily under a man's fist. He knew they had. He also knew it would never happen again, that she had a wild man with a knife standing between her and the rest of the world. They'd go down, but they'd go down with teeth bared, rabid and clawing, with the fires roaring and the winds coming down on them.

"They're coming for me, anyway. I told you I wasn't careful lately."

"Why is that, Lu?"

He sighed, and it was loud in the tractor. "This place seems perfect for two, doesn't it? It seemed small with just me, but now that you're here, it's just right."

"You're avoiding the question."

"Why don't you look in my head and tell me?"

She kissed his chin and then snuggled back into the crook of his neck. "Tell me a story?"

He was silent. Then he started to tell her a story, one of his favorites, about a little boy who cried and cried until the gods took his eyes away as punishment.

It sounded better, more right, in Mandarin, so that's how he told her. He told about the boy who wrapped a scarf around his head and went out into the world to search for his eyes.

"And did he ever find them?"

"What, you speak Mandarin now?"

"I'm watching the story unfold in your head. Or perhaps it's your heart. Either way, it's one of the most beautiful things I've ever seen."

"Then be patient. Hold on tight to your red thread, and listen to the rest of my story."

There was laughter that night, and love amidst the terror.

Outside, the police took statements from witnesses who saw a small, dark-haired girl talking to the pervy man upstairs, and then there was screaming, and a boy with a baseball cap ran into the apartment. They lifted what they could from the charred apartment. They followed bloody footprints until they couldn't follow them anymore. The wolves were closing in.

But inside the cab, it was a different story. Something beautiful. A place of peace and happiness and joy. Two people determined to enjoy each other and love until they both burned to cinders. It was a place of Chinese fairy tales and bloody hands, because no matter how hard you scrubbed the skin, you couldn't wash it out of the soul.

CHAPTER SIXTEEN

THEY DROVE UNTIL it was time to fuel the truck.

"I'll gas. How about you run in and grab some snacks?"

"Sure thing, Lu."

She kissed him and hopped out. Touched the ground with the flat of her hands stretched.

"I feel like I'm turning to stone, baby," she said.

Lu rolled his shoulders, popped his neck. "I know the feeling. Maybe we can get into town early, go on a walk or something tonight."

"Or a hunt?"

Her reflection showed her eyes glittering with a new kind of light.

It was beautiful.

"That, too," he answered, and his heart felt that now familiar piercing sensation. He knew it was love.

She ran into the gas station. Cast a longing glimpse at the sodas and candy bars, but headed straight for the ladies room instead.

Montessa finished up, washed her hands, and splashed cold water on her face. She studied herself in the mirror. No makeup. No stripper Ruby body glitter. No bruises or burns or bandages. Her face was a different sort of lovely. Eyes too large, perhaps, but they were happy and excited and full of stars and hearts and guillotines. Morning glories and ribcages shone in her eyes.

She smiled, and her reflection smiled back.

"I'm happy, I think," her reflection told her.

"I'm glad. I think I am, too."

She stepped out of the bathroom and ran into a tall man with bad tattoos.

"I'm sorry," she said and tried to step past him.

"It's my pleasure," he said and stepped in her way again.

She glared at him. "Listen. Out of my way."

He grinned back, and it made her stomach drop. "And why would I want to do that?"

She looked around. For what, she wasn't sure. Another way out. A fairy godmother. To see if anybody else saw this man, or if she was the only one.

"I've been looking for you, Montessa."

Her name. Her gaze shot up and locked on his firmly. Too firmly. She tried to back away and pressed her back against the hallway.

"How do you know who I am?"

He was enjoying it, she could see. He was riding her fear like one of the riders of the Apocalypse, thrilling to her unease. She tried to tamp the fear down, to keep it under control.

"I know all about you."

"Do you."

She felt in her back pocket for the knife, the First Kill Knife, which she had started carrying on her. Started sleeping with it. For the comfort, for the representation, because it was Lu's and now it was hers, as well. A baby born of steel. Their own, precious murder child.

"Montessa Tovar. 5'6, 115 pounds. Hair, brown. Eyes, witchy. You're Renan's whore."

She swallowed. "So Renan sent you."

"Damn near sent everyone. They're out looking for you in force. All eyes, all hands on deck."

She fingered the knife in her pocket, pulled it nearly out. "Well, you found me. Now let me go."

He shrugged, ran a hand over his shaggy hair. "Can't do it, Monty. He's paying big money for you. Big money with some extras. Can't turn you loose."

"Renan's dead. He won't be paying you anything."

The man's eyes narrowed. "Dead? Yeah?"

"Yeah. I killed him myself." He laughed, and Montessa felt the blood burn through her body, felt her mouth tighten, her eyes spark in what she thought might be reptilian. "Don't laugh at me, *boy*."

His laughter stopped, and he grabbed her wrist. "Best watch yourself, whore. Or I might not take good care of you on the way home."

"This is your last chance. Let go of me."

"No."

She used the knife and plunged it into his thigh. He yelled and doubled over, grasping at the blade. She yanked it out and plunged it into the side of his neck.

The blood. It squirted, dribbled, gushed. There weren't words. Her hands and clothes were covered, flashbacks of Emmanuel, and she felt dizzy. Turned and retched into the corner. Wiped her mouth with the back of her hand and started forward.

The man grabbed her ankle, and she went down hard, smacking her chin against the floor. She felt her teeth clack together, saw stars, and dropped the knife, which slid away from her.

"Let go!" she shrieked, and kicked him in the face. She felt his nose break under her heel, felt the grind of it, and his grip loosened.

The gas station attendant ran at them with a shotgun. "Nobody move!" he yelled. His hands shook so badly that Montessa could see the gun jittering and quivering.

"Please," she said, and held her hands up. "Please, let me stand up. Please, let me get out of this b-b-blood."

She was sobbing, crying real tears, sticky and horrible, and the attendant looked lost. "He's bleeding. I should call 911," he said. He was talking himself into it. Talking himself through it.

Montessa nodded. "Yes. Yes, do that. He attacked me with that knife there. Please, let me get up."

The dying man kicked one last time and stopped moving.

"He's dead," the attendant said. The shotgun shivered again, landed on Montessa. "You killed him."

"I didn't mean to, I swear."

"I need to keep you here until the police come."

"Yes, call them. We'll make a report."

"Stay down!"

"Please, don't shoot me."

"Stay down!" he shouted again. The attendant crept closer, resting the barrel of the gun against the top of Montessa's head. She lowered her face to the puddle of blood and sobbed.

"Please don't," she gasped. "Please don't. I'm so scared."

The attendant took a deep breath, trying to steady himself. Thought about his family or his wife or what they taught him in Gas Station 101 or any number of things. Montessa couldn't force herself to peek inside of his head, couldn't do anything but smell the blood that had just drained out of one of Renan's contacts. It was heady. Thick. She remembered the too-raw pieces of meat her daddy had tried to feed her when she was little, before Mama was dead. Before Mama became bloody bits of meat herself.

"He was gonna kill me," she said and pulled herself into the fetal position, leaving swirls of blood behind her. She sobbed into her red hands, and the clerk slowly took the gun away. "Thank you," she said, and scrabbled to her knees. She wiped her tears with the back of her bloody hand.

"Stay here. I have to call the police," the attendant said. His voice was shaking like the rest of him. Like a leaf. Like a small child. Like Montessa did the first time she clocked in at the strip club.

"Yes. Okay. Okay," she said and wiped her nose on her shirt.

The attendant turned away. Montessa picked up her knife, made it to her feet.

Lu walked in the door, saw the clerk with his shaking shotgun and his bloodied Montessa with tears running down her cheeks.

"What—" he asked but didn't get further before Montessa plunged her knife into the attendant's back. The man screamed. The shotgun went off, taking out a sad display of sunglasses on the counter. Montessa used the knife again and again and again until the man quieted.

Lu stood there, a bag of chips in his hand.

"He was going to call the cops, Lu. I killed one of Renan's men back there. Do you understand? I killed him."

She stood there, feral. Her hair glorious, her eyes wild. A savage princess. The queen of beasts. She wiped the First Kill's blade on her bloodied jeans, and Lu nearly moaned.

Her eyes searched his, looking for condemnation, looking for sweetness. He dropped the chips and put his arms around her.

"You're safe. That's what matters." He kissed her, tasting blood and tears on her lips. He kissed her deeper, holding her to his body, and she molded into him like moss to a tree, like they were always meant to be together, which he believed, of course.

"Don't ever leave me," he whispered against the other man's blood on her mouth.

"Never. You have me."

A sound, deafening, too loud too close too dead, dead, dead, and Lu grunted and fell to one knee.

The clerk lay on the floor, holding the shotgun in his hands. He closed his eyes, and the gun fell from his fingers. He lay still.

"Lu!" Montessa screamed and dropped to the ground beside her love.

"I'm okay," he said and cursed, looking at his shoulder. "We'll have to dig the shot out." He cursed again, in Mandarin this time.

Lu was raging, trying to keep the fury in. Montessa's eyes reflected the sparks coming off his skin.

"Don't hold back, baby," she said. "Let's burn this

place to the ground." She put her hand on his shoulder and closed her eyes. The wind started around them, blowing candy and engine oil and baby food off the shelves. The wind fanned Lu's flames, and they became higher and higher. "Burn," she whispered, and the building ignited. Deadly Hanukkah candles. The most exquisite of joys in the most horrible of circumstances. "Burn," she repeated and used her hand to direct Lu's flames toward the bodies on the ground. The clerk seared and sizzled. Flames danced in his open mouth, in his throat. She saw firestorms in his eye sockets.

"We have to go," Lu said, and struggled to his feet. Montessa helped him. "Now." And he started to run. Montessa ran beside him, away from the gas station, away from their truck. Montessa realized the danger they were in and gasped.

"Yeah, I know," he answered, and they ran like they had never run before. They were used to being chased by the cops. By ex-lovers, or ex-fathers, but this wasn't anything of the sort. This was a different sort of terror.

"Keep going, baby!" he yelled, and Montessa didn't say anything, but focused on her steps, on her breathing, on getting as far away as she could before the entire thing, and the gas pumps . . .

The explosion was deafening. She was knocked to the ground, hard, her breath slammed out of her. She heard the sound of Lu's beautiful bones hitting the pavement next to her, and then she heard nothing.

Nothing.

CHAPTER SEVENTEEN

SHE OPENED HER eyes and moaned. Her body hurt. Felt broken. She turned and looked behind her. The gas station was in flames, the hottest of fireballs. Lu's truck was burning as merrily as everything else.

"Oh, Lu. What did I do?"

She crawled to him, lying bloody and unmoving on the pavement. His shoulder was soaked with blood, and he had cuts on his beautiful face, but she ran her hands over his arms and legs.

He seemed whole. He seemed unbroken.

"Baby? Baby, wake up." His eyelids fluttered, and then he was on his knees, trying to stand up. Montessa put a hand on his arm. "Stay still, baby."

"We need to get out of here."

"I'll get us a car. Sit tight." She stood up and ran to the road nearby. "Help!" Montessa screamed, waving her hands above her head. "Help me, please!"

A small, white Honda stopped. A man leaned over, rolled the window down.

"There's a fire!" Montessa said, and pointed at the blazing gas station. "I just made it out, and my friend is hurt. Can you help us? Get him to the hospital?"

"Oh," the man said, and his jaw clamped shut. He blinked behind his thick glasses.

"Please?"

The man righted himself. "Yes. Of course. Climb in."

"Oh, thank you!"

She went back to Lu, put his arm over her shoulder. The man ran over to help, and they walked him to the back of the car. Lu dragged his feet, leaning heavily on the man. Much heavier than necessary.

"Thank you," Lu said weakly, and flopped into the back seat of the car. His eyes met Montessa's.

"Gladly," the man said, and leaned in to help situate Lu. "What happened out there?"

"I don't know. Everything just went up in flames," Lu said, and yanked the man fully into the car. Montessa tossed him the knife, and Lu slit his throat cleanly.

"Sorry," he whispered as the man clutched and squirmed and bled out, "but we need the car. Hope you understand."

Montessa shoved the man's kicking feet inside, shut the back door, and climbed into the driver's seat. "Anywhere in particular, my love?" she asked, pulling onto the empty road. Driving carefully. The absurdity of it struck her, and she laughed.

"Anywhere you want, Montessa. We're free. We can do anything."

She drove, wearing her long gloves of blood, with Lu and the dead man resting in the backseat. Nobody looked. Nobody noticed. The sun went down, and she followed it down the road. She turned on the dead man's radio, switched it from NPR to something with more pep. An old Styx song. "Wanted, Dead or Alive."

Montessa sang at the top of her lungs, bathed in blood and music and love.

"This is happier than I've ever been, Lulu."

"Me too, baby."

Tonight was perfect. A perfect day. Tomorrow, she hoped, would be even better.

CHAPTER EIGHTEEN

THEY DITCHED THE car and the body, cleaned themselves up as best they could, and rented a cheap room at a motel that looked the other way concerning most things. Drugs. Gunshot wounds. Blood.

Montessa used tweezers to pull the shot out of Lu's shoulder. Sweat beaded on his forehead and upper lip like dew on a rose. She had never seen anything so lovely.

"I'm sorry, baby," she said and kissed him. Bit his lip. Cleaned and bandaged his shoulder with gauze and cheap bandages purchased from a gas station she didn't burn to the ground.

"No worries. Thanks for cleaning it."

"Of course."

"Think we should take off tomorrow? Or lay low?"

Lu wrapped his good arm around her. "I think we should go to the sea. Once more. Then we can do whatever we want."

"Lulu, I feel like . . . "

"What? Time is short?"

"Yes."

"It is. That's why the sea is important. Will you go with me?"

"Gladly."

She knew what he was asking, and it wasn't just to go to the sea. It was Something Important, something of worth. He was asking her what she had been asked a million different times by a million different men, but she had never said yes. But Lu, he was different. He was where she wanted to be forever.

They slept in, and the sun was already glaring when they staggered into the motel's parking lot.

"Only a few more hours," Lu said, and Montessa stood on tiptoes to kiss him, to lick his mouth, to tell him that she had never felt this way, not once, and it was the very best and most special of feelings.

They stole a rusty, brown Camaro that didn't have locked doors. Lu concentrated, and the wires sparked just right. The engine hummed, in surprisingly good condition.

Montessa raised her eyebrows. "Nice."

And they were off. Montessa's feet on the dash, and Lu singing along with the golden oldies, the only station they could pick up.

"What if I never met you?" she asked.

"Then you'd be at home with Renan right now. Sleeping. Getting ready to dance tonight."

"I was dead, Lu. My soul was dead. My body, it's getting there. You saved me, do you know that?" She took his hand, kissed his blunt fingernails sweetly. "Thank you. Thank you for saving me. I was asleep, and you woke me up."

He didn't say anything, but his thoughts were daisies and sunshine and rainbows. The sharpest and sleekest of knives. Dahlias and straight blades.

You saved me, too, is what he thought. He thought

it with so much intensity and love that it was a firestorm in Montessa's head. The force of it blew her hair back, and she bit her lip.

So this is what it was like to have a soul mate. To be tied together with the Red Thread of Fate. It's loving somebody so much that you'll murder to be with them.

They reached the Pacific Ocean shortly before the sun was to go down.

"Come on," Lu said, and they hopped out of the car to follow the trail to the water. This beach was different, sandy and soft, and the water seemed calm.

"It isn't angry at all," she said, and leaned her head on Lu's good shoulder. "The sea is happy."

Lu wondered if she could calm it somehow, if Montessa's moods played out over the water. He wouldn't be surprised, not really. Her mama always said she was special.

"What happened to your mother?" he asked. The breeze was stiff and cold, blowing the hair back from their faces. It felt like a caress. It felt like a slap in the face. Either way he looked at it, it felt good.

"She died," she said simply, but Lu read the expressions running under her skin. Her Face Beneath A Face. *She died,* is what she said, but it was so much more than that, he realized. The sand began to tremble beneath their feet, began to lift and spin in the air in a small tornado of stinging diamonds.

"Shh," he said, and kissed behind her ear. "I didn't mean to upset you. Let's talk about something else."

The sand fell to the ground instantly, and the earth stood firm.

"I'm sorry," she said, and for a second, she looked like a little girl. Mini Montessa, with pigtails and pink party dresses and ice cream cones. Her eyes were wide and innocent. She was unspoiled. She wasn't a victim yet.

Then it all went away, and she was his Apocalyptic Montessa, a woman who had lived a thousand lifetimes in less than 30 years. He kissed her until her lips were swollen, and then he kissed her again.

"You know what takes away every pain?" he asked.

She smiled up at him, blinking with her long lashes. "Salt water," she answered. "Sweat, tears, and the sea."

Montessa took his hand and ran for the water, kicking off her shoes, laughing. Her dark hair flew in the sea breeze, and Lu found himself laughing, too. They played in the surf like lovers do. It was far too cold to be pleasant, and barely bearable. But it was their time, their moment. Lu heated the water until it was warm as blood. They played. Splashed each other. Fell down in the water, screaming and shrieking and kissing. They chased gulls, and watched tiny sand crabs crawl back and forth. They watched the sun sink into the sea, and Montessa couldn't stop staring at the color of the clouds, at the idea of the sun sinking low, low, low, until she thought she'd see steam and it would be put out completely.

"I've never seen anything so lovely," she breathed, looking at the ocean.

"Neither have I," Lu said, looking at her.

He fell on one knee, there in the Oregon sand, and took both of her hands in his. "Will you marry me?" he asked.

She sank down to her knees, as well. "Yes, my Lulu! Of course I will!"

And she flew into his arms, knocking him onto his back in the surf, and the water ran past and around them both, dragging the sand out from underneath them until it felt like they were falling. Falling like comets, like angels out of the sky. Like demons into Hell.

The stars came out. The sea continued to happily rage. It was the most perfect moment in either of their lives.

Lu reached into his wet pocket and pulled out a red string. He used the First Kill knife to cut it in half.

Montessa felt the sea water beading her face, until Lu reached over and kissed beneath her eye. She realized she was crying.

"Do happy tears taste different?" she asked as Lu carefully tied the string around her left ring finger.

"They do."

"I'd like to taste your happy tears sometime," she said, as she wrapped the other red string around his ring finger.

"I never cry."

They held hands, their new red thread wedding bands shining, and knew they were married in the eyes of God or demons, sanctified in blood and the sea, sealed with slices and blazing fires and kisses, but they were certainly married in the eyes of each other and of themselves. And really, that was all that mattered.

CHAPTER NINETEEN

L U HAD A present to give his new bride. Something special and wonderful and deeply, deeply horrifying.

"Wake up, darling."

She murmured and snuggled closer into his side. She had branches and weeds tangled into her hair like wedding flowers.

"Montessa. Wake up. Today is a new day."

She yawned and stretched and sat up. Looked around with eyes still bleary from sleep. "Lu? Where . . . ah, I remember. We slept outside last night."

They had. Several yards back from the beach, across a small freeway, up in the tree line with a few scattered rental houses here and there.

"Did you sleep sweet?" he asked.

She popped her back, winced. "I slept sweet. How's your shoulder?"

"Stiff, but not bad. The salt water hurt like a dickens last night, but I think it helped." He grinned, kissed the makeshift wedding band on her finger. "It really does heal everything."

Montessa stood up, and helped Lu to his feet. Brushed her hair out with her fingers and made a face.

"I'm a mess, Lu. I'm sorry that you don't ever get to see me prettied up."

He laughed, but she didn't. She was thinking of missed opportunities. Of things they would never see. Never have a home of their own, never have children. Something inside her ached for that, but then she remembered her own childhood, and the ache suddenly went away.

"You're beautiful to me. My wild wife. You're exactly right, and I love you for exactly who you are. And I have a surprise for you today."

The oil of tiredness fell from her eyes. They were dark and liquid, shining and wonderful. "You do? What is it?"

"We're about two hours away. I'll tell you when we get there."

"Lu! You're teasing me."

He smiled, and she kissed him. He kissed her back.

"Think of it as a wedding gift, Montessa. Something that only I can give. Are you ready? We'll head out, grab some breakfast. Switch cars and finish the trip. And then it will be something amazing."

"Let's enjoy one last walk by the sea first. I've never been there in the morning."

They held hands like any other young lovers. Dipped their toes in the freezing waves and talked about Lu's insatiable thirst for coffee and the way he had wanted to be an artist as a child.

"But my pictures kept starting on fire. I didn't understand it. And I would get so angry. Working so hard on something, and then it would burn to ash in my hands."

He didn't want to say it was the earliest allegory to

his life, that it would always be this way. He didn't want to say that the first time this happened, his mother fainted, and his father called him a demon.

Lu didn't want to say these things, but Montessa peeked into his head and knew. He was grateful that she could see these things inside of him, without words. That she knew he was like a decapitated copperhead that would strike and lash out at his own tail, chewing on his own meat in a frenzy of hurt. But Montessa kept him safe somehow. Her love was enough to keep his venom at bay, or at least, not turn onto himself.

They turned and walked from the sea.

"This will be our last time here, won't it?" Montessa asked.

Lu didn't say anything, but they both knew the answer. Knew this was the place of their wedding, and both wished it would be their burial.

"I started to fall in love with you when you told me you'd feed my body to the sea," Montessa said and laughed. She held his hand tighter. Held it to her heart, which beat with power and passion and blood, beat for the first time in her life, it felt. "I know how strange that is, Lu, but it seemed like such a kindness. Such a gift. There was so much going on in your soul, such a decency you didn't want to acknowledge."

"I do love you," he said, and his voice was rough. The words didn't come easy, even though he felt they should.

"I love you, too."

They found a car outside one of the rentals. Started it up, hopped in, and drove away without looking back. Montessa missed the scent of the ocean, the shrieking of the birds. She treasured it in her heart, in her mind.

She leaned back in the passenger seat, her feet on the dash, playing with the thread around her ring finger. She wondered about Lu, why his jaw was set in such a way. Wondered about her surprise. Wondered what it would feel like to die, when it eventually happened.

She sucked in her breath so hard that it hurt.

"What?" Lu asked her.

"Nothing, baby."

"You sure?"

"Of course." She wanted to live. She wanted to live. She wanted to live.

"You look sad."

She turned, and her smile was a soft thing, she could feel it. "How can I be sad? I only want to be with you."

He took her hand, kissed her fingers. She swallowed hard and looked at the sky.

***

They pulled into a dirty area not far from Portland. It smelled like sewers and alcohol. Meth and urine. Montessa's heart sank just looking around.

"Okay?" Lu asked.

"Yes, but what are we doing here?"

He parked the car in an alley. For a second, Montessa was afraid, the fear rising in her throat, her bones and flesh and muscle bunching together in anticipation of the attack.

Lu reached for her, and she flinched.

He pulled his hand away. "What's going on, baby?"

She shook her head. "I don't know. I'm scared. I

can't even tell you why. I just have this overwhelming sense of . . . " She gestured with her hands, but it didn't help.

"May I?" Lu asked and held out his hands.

She nodded, and he slid one to her cheek, forced her to look at him.

"I won't hurt you. Do you know that?"

She nodded again, and he kissed her. Took both of her hands and held them.

"You know how my daddy said I was a demon."

"Yes."

"And your mama said you were special."

"Do you think I'm a demon, too?"

He laughed, so sweetly and loud and with such mirth that it hurt her feelings, took her back. She pulled her hands away, wrapped her arms around herself. She was a little girl hiding in the closet then. Hiding under the bed. Behind the rhododendron bushes. Too small, too helpless.

"Baby, no. I don't think you're a demon. I'm not laughing at you. The idea of it . . . you're too sweet. Too kind. If anything, I wonder if you're an angel."

"An angel?"

He sighed, took her hand back. "There has to be balance in all things. People live. People die. If I'm a demon, you're my angel. Doing a kindness. Using your talents to better serve the world. To clean up the refuse."

She bit her lip. "The man we killed. To steal his car. He didn't do anything wrong. I've sort of been feeling bad about that."

Lu shrugged.

"You don't know that. Maybe he was a liar. A

cheater. Maybe he hurt little kids on the side. Maybe he was chosen because he needed to go. To be removed." He looked at her with intensely dark eyes. She watched the flames dancing in them. One touch on his too-warm skin and she could ignite him, she knew. Burn them both up. Go down in a firestorm of glory.

"What are you saying?" she asked.

"I'm saying to use what you've been given. To think of it as a gift. To think of yourself as an avenging angel if you need. That's why I brought you here."

She looked around the dank alley again. It smelled strongly of mold, and the dark clouds caused the light to be misty and mysterious. "An alley."

"Yep."

"This is my wedding present?"

"It certainly is."

"All right." She ran her palms down the thighs of her jeans.

"You're nervous," Lu said. He walked around and kissed her hair.

"I am. I don't know why. It's going to the very bottom of my soul. If I still have a soul. Do you think we still have souls?"

"I do." He put his arm around her, walked her down the alley. The sorrow was too much. The desperation.

"Hey," a young man said, walking down the alley. He held out a trembling hand, his arms tattooed with tracks, his face full of sores. "Hey."

It reminded Montessa of her childhood. Her mouth tasted bitter.

"It's like when I was a kid, too," Lu said. Montessa

looked at him, and he shrugged his good shoulder. "I don't have to be a mind reader to know what you're thinking."

Through the alley. Down a narrow set of stairs. They stood in a doorway.

Lu put his hands on Montessa's shoulders, whispered into her ear. "Are you ready, love?"

"R-ready for what?"

"Remember that you're strong." He used his elbow to break the window next to the grimy door. Reached in and unlocked it. Walked inside. "Come," he said and held his hand out to Montessa. She took it, stepped forward. Her white Keds crunched on the pieces of glass.

The smell. It hit home, took her back to when she was young and afraid and hurt in so many ways, bone and flesh and the soft, secret places. She clapped her hand over her mouth, trying not to throw up.

Lu watched her with intense, quiet eyes. "It's okay, baby. I'm here."

"The smell."

"What about it?"

"That brand of cigarettes. Cheap beer and that awful cologne." She went pale, whiter than white, whiter than her complexion should have allowed her to go. She gasped, grabbed Lu's hand, and staggered a bit, her head spinning.

He held her. Steadied her. Loved her and whispered to her. Thought at her with all of his might.

"I know how it feels, sweetheart. I can't smell tea leaves and incense without going right back to my father. To how scared I was, how much I hated him. It's been years, but I still feel it. He's dead, but I still feel it. But knowing he's dead? It makes it so much better."

She looked at him, terrified. Her mouth curled like a wilting flower, like a dying thing, and he watched her heart, her soul, leaving through her mouth, through her eyes.

"No," he said and shook her. "No. You're not going to disappear. You're going to do this."

"Is he here?"

"Yes."

"How did you find him?"

"I looked." He kissed her again, held her trembling body to his own. Felt the bones, so fragile. Her skin, so easily torn. Knew she was going to face a monster, a real demon. The one who started it all.

"I'm with you, baby. My Apocalyptic Montessa. I'm right here with you. Okay?"

"Okay."

He took the First Kill knife and moved it in front of her face, reflecting the dull light that came in through the broken window. Her eyes locked with his in a beautiful, perfect moment. The ground shuddered, and The-Breeze-That-Wasn't blew her hair around. He held out his palm, and a flame danced above it.

"You can do this. We can do this. It's a cleansing, angel. Take the knife."

He ran his tongue down it and handed it to her. She grasped it, squeezed his hand, and took it from him. Ran her pink tongue down the blade, as well.

Her face changed then. Became something more than what it already was. The pain and doubt and fear pushed its way to the surface, through her pores, and away from her body. There was just rage.

And hate. Brutality and an absolute absence of sympathy.

She didn't look like his Montessa at all. She was a stone goddess. Something viral. So much power and strength that she was the best predator of all, top of the food chain. He was her servant. He was her equal. He was her god, and she was everything to him. Everything.

No use for creeping. Montessa was surprised that the shattering glass hadn't brought her father to the door, but a few more steps into the dark, hopeless house and she saw why. He was passed out on a mattress on the floor. Drunk. High. Dead. Whatever.

No, not dead. His chest rose and fell, and the obscenity of watching him breathe, of watching him trap the air and pulling it, screaming, into his mouth and shoving it into this filthy, wet lungs, made her turn away. She set her jaw. Settled her stomach. Looked back at the man who was a monster to her.

"He looks so old," she said and frowned. His face was lined. His hair had turned gray. His body was soft and fat where she remembered it being mean and hard.

"And he seems smaller." She gestured at him with the knife. "He used to be so big. So tall. The room shook when he moved. But this guy?"

Her father turned over in his sleep, and Montessa jerked and then hated herself for it. Hated herself and this beast that wore the meat suit of a man.

"What are you going to do?" Lu asked. He sat on the ground, crossing his legs and looking calm, but his fingers tapped the floor and plucked at his clothes. He was so angry, so wound up he wanted to scream, wanted to take the knife from Montessa and plunge it into the old man's eyes, into his cheeks, into his groin over and over and over. To neuter him. Make him docile. There's no threat, darling, your father is standing over there in the corner with a chain around his neck. Look, he just stands there and moans. Can't see a thing without eyes. Can't say anything without a tongue. He's useless. Lame. Maimed. He's something to laugh at, to throw food at, mock. Don't you want to mock your daddy, baby? After all he did to you? Don't you?

"I want to do it quick."

Lu started. "Quick? Are you serious? You have him here, Montessa. He's right here. Helpless. Think of how he hurt you, what he did to you! You can make him suffer. Make him *suffer*."

"I don't want to."

Lu was on his feet then, bouncing from foot to foot, whispering loudly. "You'll never have this chance again. Do you realize this?" He wanted her to understand. Needed her to. "The dog needs putting down, baby," he said. He held his hand out, realized it was shaking, and stuffed it in his jeans pocket. "He's sick, and he's terrible, and he never should have walked this Earth. The only good thing he ever did was shed part of his DNA and create you. You're a wonder, Montessa. Like I said, you're the angel to my demon. Your father is an evil man who lived an evil life. Look at him. Look at him right here. Does this look like anything good to you? Does this look like the kind of man who deserves kindness? Deserves grace?"

The air became unbearably warm. Montessa breathed in, and the air choked her, scalded her lungs.

"Too hot," she gasped, and Lu closed his eyes, ran his hands through his hair. Breathed through his nose and calmed.

"I'm sorry. I'm sorry, love. I just want—"

"You want revenge for the way he treated me."

"That. And for the way he made you treat yourself. You're special, Montessa. Wonderful and lovely and amazing, but you don't know it. He made sure you didn't know it. And now look at you. At your life."

Lu's eyes were sad, sadder than Montessa had ever seen. She wanted to kiss each eyelid. To take him to a home they didn't have and curl up next to him in the garden. "I'm happy with you," she said. Her hand sought his. It was warm but not so warm it scorched. Not so warm it burned. "I just want to be with you. Do you understand that?"

"We're going to die," he said. His melodious voice was plain. Clear. "We're going to die because of what we are. Because of what they made us and what we made ourselves. He needs to be punished for that."

Montessa looked at her father, at his fat and flesh, and smelled the stench coming off his unhealthy body. "I don't have anger," she said. She sighed, and the rage left her. Now, there was just sorrow. Weariness. "He's just a sad man. I let him frighten me for so long, and I was scared of what? This broken old guy?" She handed the knife back to Lu. "Hand me the gun, please."

He did what she asked. She smiled. "I've never really had anybody looking out for me, Lu. I love you for it. I'm no angel, but I don't want to be a devil either. You're right. He's a dog, and I'm going to put him down."

She shot, twice, and her father's body jerked once.

That was all. The wheezing breath stopped. Two bullet holes showed up on his forehead, and a pool of red ran on the floor.

Her legs gave out, and she sat down heavily. Holding the gun in her hand, Montessa started to cry.

CHAPTER TWENTY

BABY," **LU SAID**, and knelt beside her. Montessa's father's blood ran over his sneakers, but he didn't care. "We have to go, baby. We can't stay here."

"I thought he was such an animal." She pulled her knees up to her chest. Wrapped her arms around them and put her head down, the gun still in her hand.

"He was a monster. You did the right thing."

"He hurt me, Lu," she cried, and rocked herself. Lu wrapped his arms around her, careful of the gun, careful of her wounded heart, careful of the pain and venom spilling from her eyes.

"It's over. You did it. You won. We won."

Years and years of misery. Of being tough. Of broken bones and dancing on swollen feet in front of men who looked at her like her father had always looked at her. And it was over. Over, with the tiniest of movements. Two short pulls on the trigger. A spasm in her pointer finger. That was it.

"Come on, baby." Lu pulled her to her feet. Ran his fingers through her hair and told her she was beautiful, that she was strong and exquisite and resilient. That she was tough and tender and amazing in every way.

He didn't use words. He didn't use his voice. He just used his heart, and she knew.

"Don't move." A voice. A shaky voice. A high, feminine voice that sounded like a martini made filthy. Lu turned around, supporting Montessa.

A woman stood in the doorway, holding a gun. She was tweaking. Her mouth moved in funny ways, her tongue running over and over and over her lips.

Montessa had the gun pointed at the stranger in seconds. "Get out, or I'll kill you," she said. Her voice was surprisingly calm. Low. Filled with deadly intent. Secretly, Lu thrilled at it. Secretly, it was what he always wanted to hear—an angel with a devil's voice, a demon's words.

"There's two of us," Lu said calmly. He held the knife in his hand. Felt its weight. Saw it shine. Practically heard it sing. "Two of us, and one of you. This won't work out well for you, lady."

"You're killers," the woman said. Her eyes went from the knife to the body on the floor. Back and forth, over and over and over.

"He's still dead," Montessa said. "You don't have to keep checking." Out of the corner of her eye, she saw her father's blood ooze out onto her shoes. Knew she'd be leaving sticky footprints again. Something for the police to follow.

"We have to get out of here," she said to Lu.

"I know," Lu said, his eyes still on the woman. "Listen, lady. The cops will be here soon, and none of us want to stick around for that. Let's leave. All of us."

"You killed John."

Montessa's voice was hard. "No loss."

The woman's face changed, crumpled in on itself

like origami butterflies in the rain. She looked lost and afraid.

Lu snorted. "You can't tell me you'll miss the guy. The way he treated you."

The woman's eyes snapped up to his face, and her hand went to her ribs.

Montessa lowered her gun slightly. "So he hits you where it doesn't show as much. He's gotten a little smarter then."

The woman took a step forward aggressively. "What do you know?" She gestured with her gun. Held it on Lu. Moved it to Montessa. Moved it back to Lu.

Lu sighed.

"I gave you a chance," he said. His eyes narrowed, and the gun suddenly went hot, scorching white, in the woman's hand. She howled and dropped it, grasping at her burned fingers. Lu stepped toward her with the knife.

Two gunshots. Montessa's signature two.

The woman fell heavily, hitting the floor with a sound that made Montessa squeeze her eyes shut. When she opened them, she saw Lu's expression. Puzzled. Uneasy. Confused and hurt.

"I'm sorry," she said. "The knife just seemed . . . I know you would have been quick. But Dad hurt her, like he hurt me. It didn't seem right to let a strange guy finish her off."

"I understand," he said, and she checked. He did. His minded tasted like salt water and compassion. And fear.

"Let's go," she said and started forward. Then another sound stopped her in her tracks. The blood fled from her face, and the gun fell to the floor.

A baby squalled. Cried. From the doorway the woman had come through.

Montessa looked at Lu. His eyebrows were high on his forehead, his mouth open. Something dark and predatory and very, very old crossed his face.

He scooped up the gun. Stepped through the door quickly. Came back. "There's a baby in there. In a pile of clothes shoved in the corner."

"It's hers?" she asked.

"Maybe. Or theirs."

"Oh. I think I'm going to be sick."

She bent over, throwing up on the floor, and Lu held her hair back. He thought about how he had done that before, when they first met, when she was tied up in the tractor of his truck.

Montessa threw up again, and he thought their meeting felt like so long ago. They were practically children then. So young and innocent.

Montessa, at least, had been innocent then. An angel.

She wiped her mouth, and Lu patted her back. She crept over to the baby and stuffed her hands in her pockets.

"We can't leave the baby here," she said.

"We can't take it to the police. So what do we do with it? Hand it to one of the junkies outside?"

"Take it and go. We'll figure it out."

She leaned down, picked up the child. Held it awkwardly like a woman who didn't know how to hold children. In any other life, she would have learned. Would have held her own sweet-smelling, round child to her breast and felt its heart beat. Known what it was like to love, to *really* love, and to be the only thing in her baby's universe. But this screeching, reeking collection of bones, only held together by sinew and newborn hatred, wasn't meant to have such a life. This child wasn't meant to be happy just as Montessa wasn't meant to be happy. It was growing up without a mommy just like Montessa had.

Because Montessa had murdered her.

"You're special, darling," she whispered to the child, and cradled it awkwardly, but the howling didn't stop.

"Shut it up," Lu said. His eyes were starting to flame. "I can't take its noise."

"I'm trying," she said and bounced the baby around in her arms.

"Just . . . come on," he said and started toward the door.

They had been there too long. First breaking the glass in plain sight, and then using the gun instead of the knife. Using it twice.

"Stupid," he whispered, and the papers on the floor smoldered, burned.

"Lu," Montessa said, cradling the baby tight.

"Stupid," he repeated, and the flames licked up the walls, onto the draperies.

"Stop it!" Montessa hurried forward, her feet slipping in the blood on the hard floor. "You're going to get us killed!"

"*I'm* going to get us killed?" Lu whirled around, his eyes glowing like the fire behind him. The baby began to squeal, and Montessa felt the child becoming uncomfortably warm in her arms.

"The baby," she said, and realized there were tears in her eyes, down her face. "Please, Lu. Baby killers go to Hell. People who orphan babies go to Hell."

Lu closed his eyes. He saw Montessa clutching the baby not like she would save it, but like it would save her soul. He saw the way her broken fingernails worked nervously on the child's red skin. He took a deep breath and grabbed her hand, pulling her past the hissing flames and through the front door.

"Hands up!"

A man on the bullhorn. A policeman outside with a gun. Several. They'd been there much too long.

Lu cursed. Raised the gun, but Montessa stepped in front of him.

"I have a baby!" she screamed. "Don't shoot! I'm holding a child!"

Lu leaned forward, rested his head against Montessa's. "I love you," he said.

Montessa turned, faced him. "What are you doing?" she asked. "Why do you sound like you're saying goodbye?"

He smiled at her, that same smile with his gloriously sharp, white teeth. Those teeth had nipped at her body, had made her smile in the dark of the night and the day. Now they broke her heart. "Take the baby to them. They won't hurt you as long as you're holding it."

"Lu."

"She's my hostage!" he screamed, and yanked Montessa and the baby to him. He pressed the barrel of the gun against her temple.

"Lu, don't do this!"

"Put the gun down! Let the woman and child go."

"Lu!"

"Her name is Montessa Tavor. I kidnapped her from Nevada. Carried her from place to place with me."

"Lu, stop it!" Montessa was crying in earnest now. The fire danced and consumed behind her. She saw her shadow, Lu's shadow, moving in fits and jerks in front of them. A strange sense of déjà vu, and she remembered watching their flaring shadows cavorting around before. Holding hands. Being together.

This wasn't that. This was different. This was a horrible, horrible thing.

"Don't do this," she begged. The baby screamed. The officers yelled and commanded. The fire crackled and guzzled and downed, and it was more than she could take in. More noise and confusion.

"You need to live, my Apocalyptic Montessa."

"I want to be with *you*. I need to live with *you*."

"You'll die. Be shot down like an animal. I can't let it happen. I tortured her!" he screamed, and pressed his gun harder into Montessa's hair. "Bled her out. Tied her up. Made her watch me kill."

The policeman closest to them tightened his grip on the gun, looking for a clean shot. Montessa could see it. Could see the way they scanned the area, the way their eyes darted around.

"I can't live without you, Lulu," she said. "I don't want to. I'm your wife. I'm made for you. You're made for me. Please don't make me do this."

"I killed her father," Lu yelled, and Montessa cringed. "Killed her father right in front of her. Killed this baby's mother. That's the kind of monster I am."

"Let her go," the officer shouted into the bullhorn. "We have a sniper who will take the shot. Let the woman and child go free."

"Do it, baby," he whispered, and kissed her behind

her ear. Her eyes fluttered closed. "Take the baby, and go to them. Tell them you were a victim."

"Lu . . ."

"I can't go to jail, do you understand? I can't be locked up in that box. Do this for me, okay, my love? Let me go."

"But . . ."

"Please!" he screamed, and Montessa jerked away. The baby howled.

"Please," he said again, softer, and the smoke brought tears to his eyes. He was backlit by the burning house, an extraordinary beast. Beauty and horror in motion.

He took a step backward, closer toward the door. Another.

Montessa felt around. Saw. Saw the officers clutch their guns, their fingers tightening on the trigger.

One more step, one of them thought. *One more and we'll have a clean shot.*

Montessa swallowed hard, looking at the sea of faces in front of her, the screams and wails of the baby, the house. She slid her foot behind her. Moved slowly. The other. Pressed her back against Lu's chest.

"What are you doing?" he asked her. His voice cracked. "I told you I can't let them take me!"

"They're not going to take you."

"Ma'am!" The voice on the bullhorn tried to sound kind, she thought. Tried to sound reasonable and supportive, but it sounded like every other man she'd ever met. Every one but her Nuclear Lulu.

"Ma'am! Walk over to us slowly. Bring the baby."

She pressed even closer to Lu. He took another step backward, and she did, as well.

"Ma'am!"

"Step inside the door," she said, and was surprised at how calm she was. How peaceful. This was what doing the right thing felt like. This was what happened when you reached the end.

"Montessa, I don't—"

"Do it."

He slid through the doorframe, heedless of the heat and flames. Disappeared inside.

"Ma'am! Now is your chance. Bring the baby out, please."

Montessa looked at the child. What an ugly thing. So small, so scared, so doomed to live a horrible, miserable life just as she had.

"Ma'am! I will not ask you again."

Only this child didn't have her father to spoil it. Maybe there was hope. Maybe this scrawny sack of ribs and vertebrae could grow up to be something . . . amazing.

"Remember that you're special," she whispered to it again, and kissed its wrinkled face. She crouched down and gently placed the baby on the ground, before she stepped through the door after Lu, chasing him down the hall into the heart of the fire. Montessa threw her arms around him and buried her face in his neck.

"Are you crazy? Are you crazy, Montessa?"

He kissed her again and again. Her scalding skin, her singeing hair, her blistering lips. The inferno wasn't affecting him, but her? She was going up in flames, just as she always knew she would. Burning as a candle. A wick. A witch.

She breathed in the smoke but choked. The hot air burnt her lungs, and she tried not to scream.

Pressed herself into her lover and thought about him instead.

Her clothes were smoking, the blood on her shoes baking and smelling like spoiled, grilling meat. Tears ran down her sooty face as they ran down his. But he was smiling.

"I love you," he said. He said it into her mouth, her face, her neck. "I love you, I love you."

She opened her eyes, which burned and stung. She licked the tears off his cheek.

"Happy tears. Tastes sweet," she said, and coughed.

Lu held his wife, kissed her fingertips and her red thread wedding ring. Kissed her long and hard and deep. He was still kissing her, holding her, running his hands over her smooth skin when he thrust the knife up under her ribs, straight into her heart.

Montessa convulsed. Shivered and shook. Blood ran from the wound, ran from her mouth. She stared at Lu and stared and stared until her pale eyes went wide, until there wasn't anything to stare at anymore. Lu cradled her body, held her close, watching her hair ignite, her clothes combust. Her flesh seared and peeled away. Still he held her.

"I love you, baby. I'll be right there."

He dropped the knife on the ground.

The First Kill knife, which was now his Last Kill knife, sparkled in the firelight. Shone. It was more perfect than it had ever been. He held the body of his wife in his bloody arms. His other half. Apocalyptic Montessa, counterpart to his Nuclear Lulu.

He took the gun from its holder, held it under his chin with one hand. Kept Montessa close with the other. Watched her ignite completely, watched her body leave this world in the grandest of manners. He'd go next. Be right behind.

A single shot. That was all.

That was all.

THE END?

Not if you dive into Mercedes' other books:

Nameless: The Darkness Comes—Luna Masterson sees demons. She has been dealing with the demonic all her life, so when her brother gets tangled up with a demon named Sparkles, 'Luna the Lunatic' rolls in on her motorcycle to save the day. Armed with the ability to harm demons, her scathing sarcasm, and a hefty chip on her shoulder, Luna gathers the most unusual of allies, teaming up with a green-eyed heroin addict and a snarky demon 'of some import.' After all, outcasts of a feather should stick together . . . even until the end.

Little Dead Red—The Wolf is roaming the city, and he must be stopped. In this modern day retelling of Little Red Riding Hood, the wolf takes to the city streets to capture his prey, but the hunter is close behind him. With Grim Marie on the prowl, the hunter becomes the hunted.

If you enjoyed this book, I'm sure you'll also like the following titles:

Wind Chill by Patrick Rutigliano—What if you were held captive by your own family? Emma Rawlins has spent the last year a prisoner. The months following her mother's death dragged her father into a paranoid spiral of conspiracy theories and doomsday premonitions. But there is a force far colder than the freezing drifts. Ancient, ravenous, it knows no mercy. And it's already had a taste . . .

Tales from The Lake Vol.1 anthology—Remember those dark and scary nights spent telling ghost stories and other campfire stories? With the *Tales from The Lake* horror anthologies, you can relive some of those memories by reading the best Dark Fiction stories around. Includes Dark Fiction stories and poems by horror greats such as Graham Masterton, Bev Vincent, Tim Curran, Tim Waggoner, Elizabeth Massie, and many more. Be sure to check out our website for future *Tales from The Lake* volumes.

Flowers in a Dumpster by Mark Allan Gunnells—The world is full of beauty and mystery. In these 17 tales, Gunnells will take you on a journey through landscapes of light and darkness, rapture and agony, hope and fear. Let Gunnells guide you through these landscapes where magnificence and decay co-exist side by side. Come pick a bouquet from these Flowers in a Dumpster.

Eidolon Avenue: The First Feast by Jonathan Winn—where the secretly guilty go to die. All thrown into their own private hell as every cruel choice, every deadly mistake, every drop of spilled blood is remembered, resurrected and relived to feed the ancient evil that lives on Eidolon Avenue.

Through a Mirror, Darkly by Kevin Lucia—Are there truths within the books we read? What if the book delves into the lives of the very town you live in? People you know? Or thought you knew. These are the questions a bookstore owner face when a mysterious book shows up.

Samurai and Other Stories by William Meikle—No one can handle Scottish folklore with elements of the darkest horror, science fiction and fantasy, suspense and adventure like William Meikle.

The Dark at the End of the Tunnel by Taylor Grant— Offered for the first time in a collected format, this selection features ten gripping and darkly imaginative stories by Taylor Grant, a Bram Stoker Award® nominated author and rising star in the suspense and horror genres. Grant exposes the terrors that hide beneath the surface of our ordinary world, behind people's masks of normalcy, and lurking in the shadows at the farthest reaches of the universe.

If you ever thought of becoming an author, I'd also like to recommend these non-fiction titles:

The *Writers On Writing: An Author's Guide* Series— Your favorite authors share their secrets in the ultimate guide to becoming and being and author. With your support, *Writers On Writing* will become an ongoing eBook series with original 'On Writing' essays by writing professionals. A new edition will be launched every few months, featuring four or five essays per edition, so be sure to check out the webpage regularly for updates.

Horror 101: The Way Forward—a comprehensive overview of the Horror fiction genre and career opportunities available to established and aspiring authors, including Jack Ketchum, Graham Masterton, Edward Lee, Lisa Morton, Ellen Datlow, Ramsey Campbell, and many more.

Horror 201: The Silver Scream Vol.1 and *Vol.2*—A must read for anyone interested in the horror film industry. Includes interviews and essays by Wes Craven, John Carpenter, George A. Romero, Mick Garris, and dozens more. Now available in paperback, as well.

Modern Mythmakers: 35 interviews with Horror and Science Fiction Writers and Filmmakers by Michael McCarty—Ever wanted to hang out with legends like Ray Bradbury, Richard Matheson, and Dean Koontz? *Modern Mythmakers* is your chance to hear fun anecdotes and career advice from authors and filmmakers like Forrest J. Ackerman, Ray Bradbury, Ramsey Campbell, John Carpenter, Dan Curtis, Elvira, Neil Gaiman, Mick Garris, Laurell K. Hamilton, Jack Ketchum, Dean Koontz, Graham Masterton, Richard Matheson, John Russo, William F. Nolan, John Saul, Peter Straub, and many more.

Or check out other Crystal Lake Publishing books for your Dark Fiction, Horror, Suspense, and Thriller needs.

BIOGRAPHY

Mercedes M. Yardley is a dark fantasist who wears stilettos, red lipstick, and poisonous flowers in her hair. She is the author of the short story collection *Beautiful Sorrows*, the novellas *Apocalyptic Montessa and Nuclear Lulu: A Tale of Atomic Love* and *Little Dead Red*, and the novels *Nameless: The Darkness Comes* and *Pretty Little Dead Girls: A Novel of Murder and Whimsy*. She often speaks at conferences and teaches workshops on several subjects, including personal branding and how to write a novel in stolen moments. Mercedes lives and works in Sin City with her family and menagerie of Strange and Unusual Pets. You can reach her at www.abrokenlaptop.com.

Connect with the Author

Website:
http://abrokenlaptop.com/

Facebook:
https://www.facebook.com/Mercedes-M-Yardley-259448987862/?fref=ts

Twitter:
https://twitter.com/mercedesmy

Connect with Crystal Lake Publishing

Website (be sure to sign up for our newsletter):
www.crystallakepub.com

Facebook:
www.facebook.com/Crystallakepublishing

Twitter:
https://twitter.com/crystallakepub

With unmatched success since 2012, Crystal Lake Publishing has quickly become one of the world's leading indie publishers of Mystery, Thriller, and Suspense books with a Dark Fiction edge.

Crystal Lake Publishing puts integrity, honor, and respect at the forefront of our operations.

We strive for each book and outreach program that's launched to not only entertain and touch or comment on issues that affect our readers, but also to strengthen and support the Dark Fiction field and its authors.

Not only do we publish authors who are destined to be legends in the field (and as hardworking as us), but we also look for men and women who care about their readers and fellow human beings. We only publish the very best Dark Fiction and look forward to launching many new careers.

We strive to know each and every one of our readers, while building personal relationships with our authors, reviewers, bloggers, pod-casters, bookstores and libraries.

Crystal Lake Publishing is and will always be a beacon of what passion and dedication, combined with overwhelming teamwork and respect, can accomplish: unique fiction you can't find anywhere else.

We do not just publish books, we present you worlds within your world, doors within your mind, from talented authors who sacrifice so much for a moment of your time.

This is what we believe in. What we stand for. This will be our legacy.

Welcome to Crystal Lake Publishing.

We hope you enjoyed this title. If so, we'd be grateful if you could leave a review on your blog or any of the other websites and outlets open to book reviews. Reviews are like gold to writers and publishers, since word-of-mouth is and will always be the best way to market a great book. And remember to keep an eye out for more of our books.

THANK YOU FOR PURCHASING THIS BOOK

9 781944 784966